CRUSADER KING

A NOVEL OF BALDWIN IV AND THE CRUSADES

CRUSADER KING

A NOVEL OF BALDWIN IV
AND THE CRUSADES

Susan Peek

TAN Books
An Imprint of Saint Benedict Press, LLC
Charlotte, North Carolina

TAN Books
An Imprint of Saint Benedict Press, LLC
Charlotte, North Carolina
2003

Lovingly Dedicated to
Our Lady,
Glory of Jerusalem

⮒ Acknowledgment ⮐

The author wishes to extend heartfelt gratitude
to Jeff Peek:
Advisor, ruthless editor, loving husband,
and the perfect knight.
Without his help, this book
could never have been written.

❧ Jerusalem ❧

"Jerusalem is the center of the world; the land is fruitful above others, like a paradise of delights. This the Redeemer of the human race has made illustrious by His advent, has beautified by residence, has consecrated by suffering, has redeemed by death, has glorified by burial. This royal city, therefore, situated at the center of the world, is now held captive by His enemies, and is in subjection to those who do not know God, to the worship of the heathen. She seeks therefore and desires to be liberated, and does not cease to implore you to come to her aid. . . ."

—Words of Pope Urban II
Clermont, France
November 27, 1095

Outremer—"the land beyond the sea"—including the
Kingdom of Jerusalem. (Shaded territory is the Crusader states.)

❧ Historical Note ❧

O N November 27, 1095, in a town called Clermont, France, Pope Urban II addressed the clergy, princes and knights of Christendom in a sermon which, unknown to himself, was about to change the entire course of medieval history. During the last several centuries, the places sanctified by the earthly life, death and glorious Resurrection of Our Lord Jesus Christ, namely the Holy Land, had been under the control of Muslims, followers of the religion of Islam, which had been founded by Mohammed in the 7th century. The Holy Land had more recently fallen into the hands of the fiercest and most fanatical of these Islamic sects, a race called the Seljuk Turks. As a result, those places held so dear to Catholics were desecrated, churches having been turned into mosques, and Christian pilgrims being robbed and often slain. The Holy Land had become a breeding ground for error and spiritual corruption. Furthermore, the insidious and false religion was threatening to spread westward.

Realizing the enormity of this danger to Holy Mother Church, the Pope made an urgent appeal to the whole of Catholic Europe, exhorting his faithful flock to lay aside all fighting between themselves and instead combine their forces in an attempt to vanquish the enemies of God and thus rescue the Holy Land from their grasp. To all those who were willing to leave behind their homes and families for the cause of this holy endeavor, the Pope offered the richest indulgences.

His proposal was received with overwhelming enthusiasm. Soon not only Clermont, but every town in Europe was resounding with the words that were to become a battle cry: "God wills it!"

Thousands upon thousands, knights and peasants alike, vowed to "take the cross" to Jerusalem. From this term came the word *Crusade,* the name by which we call this holy war and those that would eventually follow.

Within a year, four enormous armies had gathered from all parts of Europe. Like a tidal wave of humanity, these first brave Crusaders surged toward Palestine and, in 1099, reached Jerusalem itself. In a vicious and bloody battle they managed to capture this most revered city and reclaim it for Christ.

One of the armies' great leaders, Godfrey de Bouillon, was chosen to be the new ruler of Jerusalem, but he died shortly thereafter, leaving his brother to ascend the Throne as King Baldwin the First.

Victory after victory followed until the Catholics eventually gained possession of a large region of Palestine, which came to be known as *Outremer,* meaning "the land beyond the sea."

This newly restored Kingdom of Jerusalem, however, remained under constant threat from the *Infidel*—"the unbelievers," meaning the Muslims—so much so that in 1147 a second Crusade was launched to bolster the Christian position. Indeed, it would require such strengthening. For in 1137, a Muslim of Kurdish descent had been born who was to become the single most formidable enemy the Crusaders would ever have to reckon with, a man by the name of Salah-el-Din Yousouf, more commonly known as Saladin. By 1170 this military genius had made himself master of most of the ever-increasing Muslim territory surrounding Crusader lands. He would soon attain absolute power as the Turkish Sultan.

At this point in time, King Amalric the First was the Sovereign upon the Catholic Throne of Jerusalem, his heir being the young Prince Baldwin . . .

∽ **Chapter One** ∽

(The Holy Land, 1170)

KING Amalric could see his son's eyes grow wide with horror and the color drain from his face at the sight, and the Monarch's fatherly heart went out to him. After all, the boy was only nine years old and could hardly be blamed if he considered the task ahead of him the embodiment of a nightmare. But Amalric knew he must nonetheless be made to do it.

"Baldwin," he said firmly, "take the bag and do as I've bid you."

The Prince turned in his saddle to look at him with such misery that for a moment Amalric wavered and nearly relented. He felt a hand on his arm, and Sir Robert de Thierceville, the Norman knight mounted at his side, leaned closer to whisper in his ear.

"Sire, the poor child is obviously scared of them. You know he's never seen this disease before. Even grown men will run from—"

"No," Amalric cut him off. "When I die, Baldwin will be King of Jerusalem, and he must learn the compassion which Our Lord Himself showed to the sick and the poor."

Sir Robert was aware that his own ten-year-old son, Theodore, was also staring at them, frozen in his saddle. He tried again, keeping his voice low. "Your son the Prince is already an angel, Sire. He loves the poor. I really don't think—"

1

"Then he shall prove his love, and God will bless him for it." The King turned back to face his son. "Baldwin, they're waiting."

The Prince bit his lip uncertainly, but obeyed. "Yes, my lord." He took the bag of coins from his father's hand and dismounted as bravely as he could. Amalric saw him cast a pleading look at Theodore, his best friend and inseparable companion, but despite all his own virtue Sir Robert's son had no intention of going with Baldwin this time.

Baldwin took a deep breath and squared his young shoulders, determined to behave like a true knight, and strode toward the cluster of huts in the distance. He refused to let himself look back at the group of horsemen, lest they see his fear.

The inhabitants of the colony knew they themselves were forbidden to approach any closer, so none went forward to meet him. The distance seemed to Baldwin to stretch forever, and the nearer he got, the harder his heart pounded. The faces looking out at him from behind all those hooded cloaks were not the faces of men, but of monsters. Their dead flesh hung down in grisly shreds, the yellow of decaying bone visible beneath. Some had no lips, no chins, no noses. It was like a walk into the midst of the dead, yet somehow these rotting corpses were still alive.

Our Lord loves them, Baldwin reminded himself sternly with each and every step. *He made them and died for them, and I must love them too.*

Even still, the sight of thirty corrupting bodies was repugnant to him, and for a moment he had to stop, fighting off the urge to turn around and flee. But he knew his father was watching and would only make him return.

Besides, Baldwin did not want to offend the poor wretched creatures by letting them see their own prince repulsed by them. He breathed a prayer for courage and forced himself to go on.

Then, one of the lepers hesitantly came forward. Instantly the others all followed, until thirty hideous figures were surrounding Baldwin, their sunken eyes so full of trust. Someday he would be their King, and they knew it and loved him already.

But even so, none dared touch the child. None came too close.

With trembling fingers, Baldwin opened the leather pouch and saw with a shock that the coins his father had put into it were pieces of gold. The words of Our Lord came unbidden to his mind: *Whatsoever you do unto the least . . .* and he knew then what he himself would do to match his father's great generosity.

He searched their faces for the one most abhorrent and found it: a man whose eyes had been dug out by the disease. Another leper was supporting him, and it was to those two that Baldwin went first. With a racing heart he reached for the blind man's hand and placed some of the gold into his palm. Then, before either of the lepers could protest or withdraw, the Prince dropped to his knees and took the grotesque hand in his own. He forced himself to kiss it.

His stomach lurched.

"Baldwin, no!" he heard his father call out. *"You must not!"*

But the child didn't understand. He grasped the other man's hand and did the same.

"Don't touch them, son!"

He didn't hear his father's last command, nor the sudden pounding of hooves, for in his innocence he was busy whispering his own words. "My Jesus, I will do this to them all to prove my love for Thee. . . ."

He reached for the next closest hand, and then another.

∽ Chapter Two ∾

(Jerusalem, Three years later)

SIR Robert de Thierceville was returning home to the Holy City nailed in a wooden coffin, his soul finally having joined that of his wife, but their son did not yet know he was an orphan.

Theodore and Baldwin had seen the Christian army straggling back from battle against the Infidel so many times in their lives that neither of them even bothered to interrupt their game of ball in order to watch. King Amalric's knights streamed past them through the nearby field and as far as the eye could see beyond, the earth vibrating under the hooves of hundreds of heavily armored destriers, yet to the two adolescents the sight was commonplace.

It was only when the Templar army rode by that the late Sir Robert's son lost his concentration and eagerly turned to look. The Templars were not only the most feared and highly disciplined knights in Christendom, but they were monks as well, having consecrated their knighthood to God by the holy vows of poverty, chastity and obedience. To those promises they added a fourth: to fight no one but the enemies of Christ; and when they were not on the battlefield, they lived together in strict monastic brotherhood.

"Theo, catch!" Baldwin called out, amused as always by the look of awe in his friend's eyes at the sight of

5

Jerusalem's garrison of two hundred Templars.

But all of Theo's attention was fixed on Sir Odo de Saint-Amand, the venerable Grand Master of the Order, and he didn't even notice the ball as it went sailing straight over his head and landed in a nearby thorn bush.

Baldwin himself had always been impressed by the Knights of the Temple as well, and he moved over beside his friend to watch. The Templars' Rule forbade them to speak on the march, but the boys were recognized by all and greeted by more than one friendly wave as the columns filed by.

Theo glanced at Baldwin, then back at the Templars. "You'll be the King some day," he said, "but when I'm a knight, I'm going to be one of them!"

Baldwin only smiled. He believed it.

And then the last of the white surcoats emblazoned with red crosses passed by, and Theo lost interest as suddenly as he had gained it. He looked around for a moment, then asked, "Hey, Dwin? Where did you throw the ball?"

Baldwin had been scanning the field for a glimpse of his own father, but now he returned his attention to their game. "In that bush," he answered.

"Which bush? I don't see it."

"The one over there. I'll get it." Baldwin went over to the shrub and reached in among the sharp thorns.

When he managed to free their ball from the branches and pull it out, Theo saw that his hands were bleeding. Baldwin himself didn't seem to notice; he merely smiled and threw the ball back.

Theo caught it this time, and frowned. "Dwin, you cut yourself," he said.

Baldwin glanced down at his hands, surprised. "Oh, I

didn't realize. Those must have been thorns in there."

For a moment Theo just stared at him, confused. How could anyone not realize? He went over and lifted Dwin's wrists, examining the grazes. Not very deep, but certainly enough to cause pain.

"You mean it doesn't hurt?" he asked.

"No. I don't feel a thing."

"Nothing?"

"Of course not." Baldwin shrugged, almost apologetically. "Things like this never hurt anymore. I thought that's what happened when you got to be my age."

"That makes no sense. I'm nearly fourteen, a whole year older than you. And believe me, I still feel pain." Theo narrowed his eyes and wiped the Prince's blood away with his own hand to have a better look.

Baldwin thought about it for a moment, then smiling, he teased, "I bet it's something to do with being the future king. People are always talking about my blue blood." He gazed at his hands. "Though I have to admit, it looks perfectly red to me."

Theo was bewildered. Obviously kings felt pain just as much as anyone else. So what was wrong with Dwin? "You'd better tell your father about this," he said.

"Don't look so worried, Theo. I'm sure it's nothing."

"You might be sick."

Baldwin pulled his hands away, bored with the whole insignificant affair. "I don't feel sick, honestly. Now let's get back to the city. I have to get cleaned up before I can greet my father in public."

Theo hesitated. "All right," he gave in. "But promise me you'll tell him."

The Prince merely smiled, but, as always, indulged Theo. "If you insist," he agreed.

The two friends picked up their cloaks from the ground

and headed across the field, both suddenly anxious to be reunited with their fathers after such a long time apart.

In their eagerness to get home, neither of them noticed that the wagon rumbling ahead of them bore a coffin draped with the De Thierceville colors.

∞ Chapter Three ∞

THE events of the last few hours since he and Dwin had parted ways at the city gate were hardly more than a blur, and Theo's mind was still numb with shock. He clutched his cloak tightly around him against the sharp autumn breeze, unable to tear his eyes away from that gaping hole in the ground. He knew he should be praying, and he truly did try, but the words all ran together in his head and seemed so worthless. He remembered having felt this same way at his mother's funeral all those years ago. But somehow this time it was even worse, for now he was truly on his own.

Close by, a priest was reciting the burial prayers, their Latin words so familiar to Theo's ears, and the sound of them was comforting. But soon the rite would end, and this small gathering of mourners would depart to other gravesides, leaving him to face the emptiness all alone.

He had always known, of course, that this could happen someday. Every time he had seen his father put on his armor, every time he had watched him ride away from Jerusalem in the midst of the King's troops, Theo had realized that the parting might well be the last. Even still, it was hard to believe that the corpse in the ground was truly the remains of the one man he had loved and depended upon so much.

Theo was not at all sure what tomorrow would hold, nor the long lonely days and years stretching ahead.

9

Sir Robert had been of the purest blood, but was the youngest of several sons and therefore a landless knight. That was one of the reasons he had left behind his home-land of Normandy, north of France, and come on Crusade to the Holy Land. But even here he had gained no estate nor title to pass on to his own child. Theo would get no inheritance. Their home, their plot of land—everything belonged to King Amalric and had been received in return for Sir Robert's military service.

Theo didn't know what would become of him now. But at the moment none of that even mattered.

Then, as he had been so dreading, the consoling prayers of Holy Mother Church were finished and dirt was being shoveled into the grave. Gradually, respectfully, the priest and surrounding knights started to leave, each offering his gentle condolences and assuring Theo that his father had died bravely. But these men were hardly more than strangers to Theo, people he had seen often enough yet had never spoken with, and their words, although sincere, did little to ease the crushing burden of sadness.

How long he stood there, watching the rhythmic swinging of the shovel as if in a dream, he had no idea. It was only when he heard the sound of approaching horses that he looked up. Even at a distance there could be no mistaking that little group of riders. It was part of the royal retinue, with the King himself in their lead.

They reined in a few yards away and the Monarch alone dismounted. Theo wasn't certain what he was expected to do, but relief flooded through him when he spotted Dwin in their midst. The Prince gave him a look which said more than any words ever could, and for the first time in all these hours Theo didn't feel quite so alone.

King Amalric came over and clasped an arm around his shoulders. The strength and calm dignity of the

Monarch were reassuring, and for a long moment Theo just leaned against him, grateful to hide his face in the material of the King's heavy cloak.

"I'm so sorry, my boy. Your father was one of my best and truest knights. He will be mourned by many."

Coming from the Sovereign, these words meant more than all the others Theo had heard that day. He knew he should say something in reply, but he was afraid to speak, lest his voice break.

"Come away, Theodore," the King said at last, urging him toward the waiting horses.

Theo didn't want to go. It seemed so horrible to just leave his father's grave all alone like that. But he nodded anyway, only too relieved to have someone else tell him what to do.

Chapter Four

BALDWIN was grateful that the meal, at least, was finally over. It had been the longest banquet he'd ever had to sit through in his entire life, and all he wanted was to escape to his room alone and look at it again. Maybe he'd just imagined it, he told himself. Maybe it was only part of last night's horrible dream and hadn't really happened at all.

He was dying to go and look, just to reassure himself it wasn't true.

But, to his utter misery, he knew he still had a long evening ahead of him before he could take his leave from the banquet hall. The King always insisted on his son's presence in court like this, and Baldwin knew there was nothing he could do about it.

With the clearing of the tables, the barons and ladies had broken up into noisy little groups, scattered throughout the room, and those who weren't talking were distracted by the music of the minstrels. Well, the Prince might not be allowed to actually leave, but at least he was being ignored for now. He glanced around for Theo amongst the many pages, but saw that his friend was busy serving the wine.

After the death of Sir Robert all those months ago, King Amalric had taken the homeless boy into his own household as a page. Baldwin knew it hadn't been easy on his friend, but Theo had taken it well. And they still had each other.

Baldwin got up from his place next to his father's chair and wandered over to the blazing fire. From the way everyone was dressed he assumed it must be cold, although he didn't feel the wintery chill himself. Still, if he *had* been cold, then the hearth would be the natural place for him to go, and he didn't want anyone here to suspect he was somehow different from everybody else.

He turned his back on the room and reached out his hands toward the flames. He felt their heat no more than he felt the cold, but he was becoming good at pretending. It was silly, of course, to be standing here warming his hands when he already had gloves on, but he hoped no one would notice.

He had kept them on all day, those heavy gloves, even during the meal. A few of the pages had looked at him curiously when they had served his food, but none of them had commented. That was one good thing about being a prince: no one dared interfere with his private affairs. If he chose to eat with gloves on, fine. That was his business, not theirs.

But every time Baldwin thought about it, he felt his heart clench with fear. His hands. The way they had looked this morning! For several weeks now there had been a few strange little lumps appearing. He had forced himself to ignore them, praying they would just go away. But they hadn't, and now he was becoming scared. Really scared! Part of one fingertip, which had been infected, had fallen off this morning. Fallen off, just like that! And the ugly sores were spreading.

He took a deep breath and tried not to think about it. *Everything will be all right,* he told himself firmly. *It'll grow back. It has to!*

"Do you have any idea," squawked his sister suddenly from behind him, "how ridiculous that looked? If I were you, I would have died of embarrassment!"

Baldwin's heart skipped a beat. Had Sibyl seen? Had she actually seen what had happened this morning?

He tried to stay calm, although his pulse had started racing, and turned around to face her. He forced a smile. "What are you talking about, Sibyl?"

Her eyes traveled to his hands, and Baldwin practically stopped breathing. "Eating with gloves on!" she scoffed. "I've never seen such a stupid thing in my life! Are you trying to become the court jester, or what?"

Despite himself the Prince let out a sigh of relief. Maybe his sister didn't know after all.

"Well?" she provoked. "What did you do that for?"

He tried to think of something reasonable to say. "I wanted to. Haven't you noticed it's cold in here?" Lame, but at least it wasn't a lie.

His reply, however, only disgusted her. "What kind of a wimpy king are you going to make?" she accused. "Can't even put up with a chill in the air! Even the old ladies in here can do better than that!"

Baldwin said nothing. His father had told him that a man must never, ever take up arms against a lady, no matter what the circumstances. Well, arguing was a form of fighting, wasn't it? Besides, he knew poor Sibyl was only jealous of him. That was all there was to it. She was two years older and hated him because he was heir to the Throne and she wasn't.

She put her hands on her hips and was just about to have another dig at him when suddenly a page came rushing up with a broom. He ignored the Prince and spoke directly to the Princess instead.

"Your Highness, have no fear! If you would just step aside for a moment, I shall be honored to kill him for you."

Sibyl's eyes widened. For once in her life she was speechless.

It was all Baldwin could do to keep a straight face. What on earth did Theo have up his sleeve this time?

"You may want to close your eyes," Theo continued as charmingly as he could. "I'll try not to splatter too much blood, but, well, I can't guarantee anything."

Sibyl managed to recover her voice. "You're going to kill my brother for me?" she asked in disbelief. "Right here in front of everyone? With a *broom*?!"

"Oh no, Your Highness," Theo answered solemnly. "I was talking about that rat that just ran under your skirt a minute ago."

The Princess let out a shrill screech and leaped into the air. Then, with no idea how ungraceful she looked, she bolted away as fast as her legs would carry her.

For a few seconds both boys were too overcome with laughter to speak. Then finally Baldwin glanced around. "I don't see a rat," he said.

"Of course not. She just left."

"Theo!"

The page tried his best to look contrite. "Sorry, my lord."

"You really shouldn't have done that, you know."

"Of course not, my lord."

"It was most unchivalrous and ignoble—"

"Yes, my lord."

"—and I wish I'd thought of it myself!"

Theo grinned. "I'm sorry," he repeated. "You just looked like you needed rescuing. I couldn't think of any other way to get rid of her." He put the broom down and moved closer to the fire to warm his own hands. Then his amusement disappeared, and he lowered his voice so no one else would hear. "You've been very quiet all day," he said.

"There's something wrong, isn't there?"

Baldwin hesitated, and his eyes traveled again to those heavy gloves and the terrible thing they were hiding. "Yes," he answered truthfully.

"Do you feel like telling me? I mean, you don't have to, but you can if you want."

Yes, Baldwin did want to. "I'm scared, Theo," he whispered. "It's . . . it's getting worse."

Theo knew exactly what he was talking about. "How much worse?" he asked.

The Prince bit his lip. "Lots."

Theo paled ever so slightly and turned to look at him. "Don't be scared, Dwin," he said softly. "It's not that same disease. That was three whole years ago! This is something else, and it'll just go away by itself. I'm sure it will."

"That's not what the doctors told my father."

"I don't care what the doctors told him. They were wrong!"

Baldwin felt that familiar knot of fear in the pit of his stomach. "What if they weren't?" he asked. "What if I truly did catch it?"

Theo turned away to stare at the flames and was quiet for such a long time that Baldwin started to wonder if he had heard. But finally Theo answered, and his voice was unsteady. "Even if you did catch it, it'll never get as bad as what we saw."

"How do you know?"

"I just do!" Theo looked at Baldwin again, and Baldwin could feel his friend's gaze searching every inch of his face for reassurance that the disease wasn't really there. "Come on, Dwin," he said at last, "anyone can see you're turning out just like your father. Diseases like that simply don't attack princes—that's all there is to it."

"But what if—"

"Just stop it, will you?" Theo begged. It was obvious he was scared too but was trying not to show it.

Baldwin suddenly felt like a coward. After all, his friend had carried even heavier crosses since the death of his father, Sir Robert, yet had been so courageous about it. Surely the son of a king could have at least as much courage as the son of a nobleman!

He took a deep breath and forced himself to smile. "You're right, Theo," he said. "I'm getting all worked up over nothing. In a few months it'll all disappear, then we'll both laugh over this whole stupid thing."

Theo tried to smile back. "That's what I've been trying to tell you for weeks."

But deep in their hearts, the two boys both knew they were wrong.

∽ **Chapter Five** ∾

THEO was going to suffocate to death. He was sure of it. How he was ever going to get used to having his head stuffed inside this metal box with no air, he had no idea. Yet there must be a way to keep breathing in here, or every knight in the Kingdom would drop dead before even meeting Saladin's army.

He shifted uncomfortably in the huge saddle and looked through the narrow eye slits at his friend mounted beside him. Behind his own helm, Baldwin's eyes were amused. Well, all very fine for *him,* Theo thought! Baldwin had been training in arms since he was old enough to sit on a horse. That was different—Dwin was a prince! Theo himself had had to wait until the King made him a squire before he was allowed to start learning this stuff.

His horse was becoming impatient and started to prance. It wasn't easy to keep the thing in check, and yet this was only a baby warhorse! But Theo was as determined as his mount to be the one in charge, and he held the reins as tightly as he could.

Sir Eudes, the veteran knight whom King Amalric had entrusted with the task of teaching his son, now asked, "Are you ready, Your Highness?"

"Yes."

"And you, Theodore?"

Theo wasn't too sure, but he answered anyhow. "Yes, my lord."

18

"All right. Now just remember, hold your lances low enough to keep them steady, but not so low as to miss your target."

The boys both nodded, and Sir Eudes stepped out of the way of their horses. Theo knew he was the envy of every squire in the kingdom. No other boy had the privilege of training with the Prince himself. Well, he wasn't going to disappoint the King, even if it killed him. And, to be honest, he was starting to wonder if it might. . . .

He trotted his horse to one end of the practice yard, while Baldwin went to the opposite. Then they reined their mounts around to face each other. Theo knew there was almost no chance of really getting hurt. Their lances were blunted, their bodies each protected by an aketon, the thick padded tunic which knights wore beneath their mail. But even still, it was unnerving to have to charge at each other like this.

Funny, he thought—they'd been playing battle games together ever since he could remember, but somehow it all seemed so different with Sir Eudes standing there watching. This was serious. Official.

He positioned his shield and couched the long wooden lance in the crook of his arm. It was harder to balance than he had thought it would be, yet he knew a real one was much, much heavier and longer than this toy. Across the field he could see Baldwin preparing as well.

Then Sir Eudes gave the signal. Theo held his breath and dug his heels into the horse's sides. The charger bolted forward. It wasn't the horse itself which was hard to control. No, he'd been on galloping mounts thousands of times. Rather it was the restricted vision, the inability to get enough air, and the difficulty of balancing both lance and shield which made it all so awkward.

Then, before he knew it, the other horse loomed up in

front of him and he felt a jolt. There was a sound of splintering wood, and for a second Theo had to struggle to stay in the saddle. Then suddenly it was all over and he continued to ride across the yard.

Well, that hadn't been too bad at all. No big deal.

The only problem was, Theo couldn't figure out if he had hit Dwin or if Dwin had hit him. He had no idea in the world!

He reined in, and his mount slowed to a stop at the far end of the field. He looked at the tip of his lance.

Perfectly intact.

He sighed.

The Prince had already turned his horse to the center of the yard, where Sir Eudes was waiting for them. Theo wondered if he himself would be reprimanded for having done such a poor job. Well, there was no way out of it. He nudged his charger into a gentle lope and rode back to the middle.

But before their mentor had a chance to say anything to either of them, a group of barons walked into the practice yard. Theo was surprised to see who they were: the King's own men. Sir Eudes excused himself and went over to meet them.

Count Raymond of Tripoli, King Amalric's cousin, was at their head. Next to the King himself, Tripoli was the single most powerful man in the realm. For some reason Theo had never trusted him. He always looked as if he had something to hide.

Jocelin de Courtenay was there too: Dwin's uncle on his mother's side and the Senechal of Jerusalem.

Other barons had come as well, all of them holding the highest positions at court. They were speaking quietly to Sir Eudes, and Theo noticed a few glances cast in their own direction. He wondered whether he was expected to leave. Something important must be going on, and maybe they wanted him out of the way.

Surely Dwin would know what he was supposed to do. He nudged his horse closer to ask.

Baldwin was reaching up to take off his helm, and despite himself Theo held his breath. It was silly, of course, but every time Dwin took the thing off Theo half-expected his face to be . . . well, sick. Like his hands.

But it wasn't.

No, Dwin looked exactly the same as he always had. The perfect prince.

Relieved, Theo let out his breath and reached up to free his own head from that instrument of torture. He could feel his hair plastered to his forehead, the sweat trickling down into his eyes. He peeled off his gloves and wiped his face.

Dwin, however, kept his own gloves on. He always did. Theo never saw him without them, nor did he ever roll up his sleeves anymore. Not since that one day so many months ago when this whole terrible thing had started happening. Theo tried not to think about it and instead asked, "Should I leave?"

"No, I don't think so," Baldwin answered, his eyes on the group of barons. "They'll probably be gone in a minute. I'm sure it has nothing to do with us."

"Then why do they keep looking over here?"

Baldwin shrugged, unconcerned, and wiped his sleeve across his brow. He, too, was sweating in the scorching Jerusalem heat, and Theo wondered how strange it must be for him to know he was sweltering yet not feel it.

Then they both saw Sir Eudes returning, his face white beneath the blackness of his beard. He stopped before Baldwin's horse and, for the first time ever, looked unsure of himself. Then he did something he had never done to his pupil before. He bowed.

He actually *bowed*!

Theo's heart skipped a beat.

Sir Eudes cleared his throat and said gently, "Sire, I'm afraid these men have some very sad news for you. Perhaps you should go with them."

Baldwin froze in his saddle, and Theo knew he had heard it too. They both had.

Sir Eudes had called Baldwin "Sire," the title of address given to none but the King alone.

∽ **Chapter Six** ∽

COUNT Raymond of Tripoli just could not believe his luck. For years he had been wondering when his chance would finally come. And now here it was, practically tumbling into his lap. It was just as well he was supposed to be smiling as he stood here beside the throne watching all the barons and knights pay homage to their new monarch, for it would have been impossible right now to hide his pleasure.

A thirteen-year-old boy—a mere child!—having been crowned this very day. What an incredible stroke of fortune! With Amalric alive, Tripoli hadn't stood a chance in a million of overthrowing the Kingdom. But now it was going to be utter simplicity! He had always known, of course, that he would never become the King of Jerusalem himself. No, that was a dream which, alas, could not be so easily fulfilled. But Tripoli was willing to settle for less, if need be. Money. Lots of it. Land, too, and the power that would go with both. Not quite as tantalizing as the Throne itself, he had to admit, but certainly better than the limited wealth he now possessed.

With that in mind, he had already struck a secret deal with Saladin, the Turkish Sultan. Help the Muslims take Jerusalem, and he himself would be rewarded with more gold than he could probably even imagine. And Tripoli could imagine an awful lot of gold.

He had been studying every face, for well over two

hours, as the nobles of Outremer came, one by one, and knelt before King Baldwin the Fourth to swear their Oath of Fealty. The formula was exactly the same for each man, just a string of fancy words, whose value, Tripoli knew, lay only in the heart of the speaker. What he was trying to figure out was just how many of these knights really meant what they said. Which among them would faithfully serve this child and bend to his every command?

No doubt many of them would. It was obvious that Amalric had trained his young son well and the boy was already beloved by the people as their king. For at age thirteen Baldwin was old enough by law to reign without a regent. But there were a few in this vast crowd whom Tripoli might be able to turn against him.

The Lord of Kerak, for instance. His real name was Renaud de Chatillon, but everyone called him the Hawk. And it wasn't because of his looks, either. Kerak would bow to no one, and had spent a lifetime proving it. An outlaw and a pirate, he even had his own private army. The only reason King Amalric had put up with the rogue was because he was such a fearless warrior.

Hmm, yes. Perhaps Kerak could be useful in dethroning this young Baldwin.

The only problem was, of course, that the Hawk hated Tripoli as much as he hated everyone else.

Oh well, there were still others . . .

Tripoli's gaze traveled across that sea of faces gathered in front of him and came to rest on Lady Agnes de Courtenay. Now there was an enemy of the King! Baldwin's very own mother. Amalric had banished her from Jerusalem shortly after their son had been born, and she had never even seen Baldwin again until this day. It was obvious by the hardness in her eyes that her hatred for her husband had overflowed to include her son as well. Perhaps it was because he looked and acted so very much like his father. At any rate, she despised him.

Tripoli knew that Lady Agnes was herself bent on power. A headstrong and haughty woman, she had been trying for years to undermine the authority of the Crown. Many influential noblemen in the realm were on her side, and resentment against Baldwin was exactly what Tripoli needed. Create an anarchy, and Saladin could easily conquer this Kingdom.

And of course there was always the gorgeous Princess Sibyl. She could certainly be counted on to stir up trouble! Everyone knew she envied her little brother and would do anything—absolutely anything!—to sit upon that splendorous throne herself.

Tripoli nearly laughed. If only poor Sibyl realized how close she really was. For he knew a secret which she did not. Her brother could never get married, could never have a child of his own to inherit the Crown when he died, and Sibyl was actually his heiress! Next in line for the Throne, and the girl didn't even know it!

Indeed, Amalric had kept the incredible secret well guarded. Even his own daughter had not been told that her brother had contracted leprosy.

King Baldwin was actually a leper! And no one here realized it!

Tripoli felt his smile broaden. Just wait till the people found out about this! The boy would be deposed by public outcry and shunted off to a colony somewhere, never to be seen again. Princess Sibyl could not become Queen until she was married, so the Kingdom of Jerusalem would be left without a sovereign. Absolute anarchy!

As a matter of fact, the more Tripoli thought about it, the more stunned he was by how easy this was going to

be. He would have hardly anything at all to do to help
Saladin take these lands. Just let things run their natural course, and Outremer was bound to crumble to
pieces.

And all that Turkish gold would be waiting for him,
just begging him to come and claim it.

~ Chapter Seven ~

BALDWIN wondered if he was ever going to get used to this, sitting at his father's place at the high table. After nearly a month, he still sometimes forgot and went to the wrong chair. But his attendants were always so patient, reminding him where to go, and for that he was relieved. Still, Baldwin felt as if he had taken something which shouldn't belong to him.

He had always known, of course, that he would someday be King, but he had never dreamed it would be so soon. No, he had just assumed that he would be a grown-up when his father died and left him with the weight of the entire Kingdom upon his shoulders. He begged God every day—countless times a day!—to make him a good and just ruler, to help him in all these immense responsibilities which had so suddenly fallen into his lap. His father had tried to prepare him for this during his whole life, but it was so different to actually do it in reality. And he missed his father so much!

He finished his meal, and a page came to refill his cup. Baldwin shook his head, unwilling to drink too much of the strong wine. Besides, it was the time of evening when the gates of the city were always locked for the night, and he liked to supervise this function whenever he could, as his father had done before him.

He silently said his own after-meal grace and rose to leave. Instantly every other person in the room stood up as well, and all conversation ceased. This, too, he would have to get used to. His attendants draped his royal robe around his shoulders and stepped forward to accompany him, but Baldwin motioned for them to stay behind. He didn't need a flock of pages trailing after him every single hour of the day! Instead his eyes traveled to the small group of squires at the far end of the hall, and he indicated for Theo alone to follow.

As Baldwin crossed the floor of the great hall everyone bowed respectfully, and it wasn't until he had stepped through the door and out of their presence that they resumed their seats.

He waited for Theo to join him, then said, "I'm going up to the walls. Want to come?"

Theo smiled. "You bet I do."

The garrison of Templars were the ones in charge of guarding the city, and once those gates were locked each evening, no one could get in or out without the consent of the Order's Military Marshal, Sir Gerard de Ridford.

Together the two boys made their way through the palace and into the open air. "You know something?" Baldwin asked after a minute.

"No. What?"

"I'm starting to wish you didn't want to become a Templar once you're knighted."

Theo looked at him, surprised. "Why?"

Baldwin sighed. "Because my father's arrangements for Sibyl's marriage didn't work out, and now it's up to me to find a husband for her. You would have been my first choice."

Theo stopped walking and stared at him, stunned. "Hey! And I thought I was your friend!"

Baldwin nearly laughed at the look on his face. "You are my friend, dummy," he reassured with a grin. "Don't you realize I'm offering you the highest honor in the Kingdom?"

"Really? You could've fooled me."

"Don't you get it? Think. When I die someday, Sibyl will become the Queen. And that makes her husband the next King of Jerusalem."

Theo just stood there, dumbfounded, as the implication sank in. Baldwin, however, started walking again and Theo hurried to catch up. "Wait a minute," he objected. "That's not how it works. Your oldest son inherits the Throne, not your sister."

Baldwin felt that familiar sickening dread. "Not in my case," he said quietly. "I'm never going to have a son. I can't make anyone marry me."

"What a crazy thing to say! You, of all people, can take your pick. And it's not just because you're the King either. Believe me, Dwin. I know about these things."

"But I'm sick, Theo. Remember? And it's only going to get worse. Sometimes I wish you'd just stop pretending I'm normal because—"

"You *are* normal, Dwin. You've caught some kind of infection, that's all. Besides, I ask God every single day to make you better, and He always hears our prayers."

Baldwin fell silent. There was no point arguing about God answering prayers in His own way. He knew Theo was sincere. But it had been a long time since Theo had seen the way his hands and arms actually looked.

He sighed and glanced at his friend. It was obvious that poor Theo was suddenly depressed. Baldwin forced a smile and gave him a playful punch. "Come on," he teased, "what do you say? Want to be the next King or not?"

Theo couldn't help it. He had to laugh. "Believe me," he answered, "I'd rather be the lowest serf who cleans the latrines than the mighty nobleman who gets stuck with your sister! Even if she is gorgeous and comes with a free Kingdom."

Now Baldwin laughed as well. "All right," he conceded. "Point taken. I'll let you off. Go ahead and be a monk."

"You know I'd make a rotten king anyhow."

Baldwin could have argued with that, but he didn't. He knew he would just have to choose another virtuous nobleman. Possibly one of the Ibelin brothers. Or better yet, that William de Montferrat, the one called Sir William Longsword.

They reached the city walls in silence and stopped to watch the locking of the gates below. Baldwin understood why his father had gone nearly every evening to see this. It was a sobering reminder that they were living in a state of constant warfare. They were never safe, never able to just go to bed without wondering if the city might be attacked as they slept. Saladin was always out there, waiting.

"Hey, Dwin," Theo spoke up, pointing into the distance. "Someone got locked out."

Baldwin had already spotted the lone knight galloping across the bleak desert sands. "I see him," he said. "The Templars will take care of it." They always did. It was their job to find out who the man might be and why he desired to enter the city after hours.

Sure enough, by the time he arrived, a pair of the warrior monks were waiting for him on the wall just above. The knight reined in, and even from where they stood the two boys could see how desperate and exhausted he looked. He had obviously ridden at great speed for a long time.

"Let me in!" he gasped, addressing the Templars.

"The gates are already locked," one of them called

down. "First state your business, and we'll speak to our Marshal."

"I bear a message of utmost urgency for His Majesty the King. Please, I must see him!"

Before the Templars could reply, Baldwin moved closer and called down to the man himself. "I am the King, Sir Knight. What have you to say?"

The messenger looked up, confused for an instant, and Baldwin realized that the man had forgotten it was no longer Amalric who was king, but his son. The knight, however, recovered quickly and wasted no time. "My liege, the city of Aleppo is under attack. The Christian population there is large. They entreat you to send reinforcements."

Before Baldwin had time to say anything, Theo unintentionally blurted out, "Aleppo! That's hundreds of miles north! We could never get an army there in time!"

The knight was waiting for the King to answer.

Baldwin whispered a silent prayer for help, then turned to the Templars. "Open the gates," he ordered, "and let this man in."

✑ Chapter Eight ✑

"**M**OTHER, you're frowning. What's the matter? Haven't you ever even seen an army preparing to ride out?"

Lady Agnes de Courtenay turned to glare at her daughter, standing beside her at the window. She quite liked Sibyl, from the little she'd gotten to know of her these past few weeks, but the girl could be obnoxious when she chose.

Of course she had seen armies before. There was no point even answering such a patronizing question! Instead, she decided to ask a few questions of her own. After all, perhaps her daughter knew the truth behind these strange rumors floating about the court lately.

"Sibyl, dear, tell me," she began. "Is your brother ill in any way?"

Now it was the Princess's turn to frown. "No, not that I'm aware of. Why?"

"Oh, just wondering. I can't help but notice that he tires easily. More than most boys his age."

Sibyl reluctantly tore her eyes away from the handsome knights gathering in the fields outside the city walls and looked at her mother. Actually, now that she thought about it, Baldwin did seem to have less energy than the other boys she knew.

"He's just lazy," she answered. "Wants his servants to do absolutely everything for him."

Lady Agnes grunted. "Just like his father. Put a crown on his head and suddenly he owns the world and everything in it."

The Princess returned her gaze out the window, uninterested in hearing her mother's string of complaints for the millionth time. All men were pigs, she had already figured that out. She didn't need her mother to tell her!

But to her relief, for once the Countess de Courtenay didn't go on about King Amalric. Instead she changed the subject back to Baldwin. "Those gloves," she said. "Why does he always wear them?"

Sibyl smiled, amused. "He's been doing that for ages. Says the cold bothers him."

"Heavens, child! It's sweltering outside!"

The Princess shrugged. "Don't ask me. He's just strange. Trying to get attention, I bet. As if a prince doesn't get enough attention already!"

"A king, dear."

"Of course. I forgot. A king." The very word brought a rush of envy, and suddenly Sibyl didn't feel like watching the army gather anymore. It was her brother's army now, and that was so different from when it had been her father's.

She knew it was wicked of her, and she'd probably have to confess it as a sin, but she couldn't help hoping that Baldwin would be killed in Aleppo. Then she would be the Queen!

Lady Agnes persisted with her prying. "So he doesn't wear gloves to hide anything?"

"Of course not. What a ridiculous thought, Mother! What could he possibly be trying to hide?"

Well, it was obvious. Her daughter knew nothing of these stories. Should she tell her or just let it drop?

The Countess considered for a long moment, then

decided to tell. After all, Sibyl had every right to know that she shouldn't touch her brother anymore—although leprosy wasn't as contagious as most people believed, and relatively few people were able to catch it at all. Any educated doctor could tell you that. Some people were just susceptible to the dreadful disease, while many were not.

Yet even so, Lady Agnes wouldn't want both of her children transformed into ugly monsters. Gracious! What would people say?!

She smiled sweetly. "Sibyl, darling," she began, "I think there's something you really ought to know . . ."

✐ Chapter Nine ✐

THEO sat as tall as he could in his saddle as he cantered past the sea of warhorses and colorful banners toward the front of the huge army. He still couldn't believe it: only fourteen years old and he was actually going to ride off to his first battle. He'd spent his whole life waiting for this day, when at last he could fight for God's glory and the cause of the Kingdom.

He knew he had almost reached the vanguard now, for he was passing the Hospitallers, the Knights of St. John. Like the Templars, they too were a religious-military Order, and Theo had always been impressed upon seeing the columns of monks, their stark black armor broken only by the white cross upon each chest. Yet even still, he had never found them quite as formidable as the Knights of the Temple, and as soon as his horse was alongside those white-clad warriors—this time the cross was emblazoned in red—he felt his pulse quicken.

They reminded him so much of statues, mounted there in perfect silence, so calm and confident. And to think that he was going to be riding in their midst, right there beside the King himself! Even his own father had never had such an honor.

Theo could see now to the very front, where the Standard of the Kingdom was fluttering in the breeze and, behind it, the Bishop of Jerusalem sat upon a donkey. Dwin was there too, of course, in a surcoat of gold and mounted on the most magnificent stallion Theo had ever seen.

For a moment he felt uncertain and slowed his own horse to a trot. Maybe he should have asked Baldwin first before so boldly barging his way up to the front like this. He hesitated, suddenly feeling awkward in his ill-fitting coat of mail. He had never worn armor before. How come Dwin looked so majestic and natural in it, while he himself only resembled an overstuffed metal dwarf?

But his uncertainty only lasted for an instant. After all, the King was his best friend! How many thousands of times in their lives they had both dreamed of this moment, longing for the day they would ride side-by-side to fight Saladin. Before he had time to change his mind, Theo dug his heels into the charger's sides and rode straight in front of the Templar line. He didn't stop until he had reached the King.

Baldwin was speaking with Sir Odo de Saint-Amand, the Grand Master, and on his other side sat Sir Gerard de Ridford, the Order's Marshal and supreme military commander. Theo had seen the two men countless times in his life, but he'd never dared speak to either of them.

The moment they saw him, their conversation ceased. Theo realized that, indeed, the entire Templar army was watching to see what business this brazen young squire could possibly have way up here at the front of their troops. He tried to ignore their gazes and instead addressed his friend. "Sire," he said respectfully, "I beg the honor of riding at your side, as the lowest of your attendants."

Baldwin was silent for a moment, then nudged his stallion forward closer to Theo's. He lowered his voice. "You're not supposed to be here," he whispered.

"I know. But I didn't think you'd mind. I want to stay with you, not back there riding with a bunch of knights I've never met before and—"

"I don't think you understand, Theo. You're not supposed to be here, *at all*."

Theo just looked at him, bewildered.

Baldwin wavered, obviously hating what he was about to say. Yet he said it nonetheless. "I'm sorry, but you're not coming to Aleppo with us."

"Not coming? What do you mean? Of course I'm coming!" Dwin wouldn't really ride off without him! Impossible!

"Theo, you're only fourteen. I can't let you."

Theo couldn't believe this. "I'm nearly fifteen! That's older than you, and you get to go!"

"I have to," Baldwin answered. "I'm the King. It's the only reason, otherwise I'd be left behind too. You know it's true."

"Dwin, come on! You can't be serious!"

Baldwin drew in a breath and cast a glance around them. Then he looked back at his friend. "Go home, Theo," he ordered. "You're too young and I'm not going to let you get killed." Before the other boy could object, he added softly, "Everyone's watching this, you know."

Theo's gaze jerked back to that silent sea of Templars, and he realized that Dwin was right. He had actually forgotten about them, so absorbed was he in his own motives. Yet all those knights were taking this in, watching to see how well their new king could handle a mere squire and make him obey.

Instantly Theo felt his cheeks start to burn.

But before he had a chance to say anything else, Sir Odo de Saint-Amand moved his own mount forward and intervened. "My son," he said, gently laying a hand on

Theo's arm, "we've been fighting this Crusade for nearly a hundred years already, and the end is still nowhere in sight. Be patient for yet a few more years. Someday you'll be knighted, and I can assure you there will still be plenty of Turks out there waiting for you."

Theo wasn't sure what to say. He had never felt so small, so crushed, in all his life. Yet he didn't want all these Templars to see it.

Sir Gerard de Ridford moved up to join them as well, but he had nothing of the Grand Master's kind and paternal manner. Instead he pierced Theo with a look of disdain, then turned impatiently to the King. "Sire," he said, "the entire army is kept waiting."

Theo cringed. He didn't dare look at his friend. "May God protect you, Sire," he forced himself to say, "and bring you safely home." Then, before Baldwin could answer, he jabbed his spurs into his horse and galloped out of the army's way. He didn't want Dwin to know just how devastated he really was.

No sooner was he gone than the Marshal raised a hand to give the signal, and the Templar vanguard moved forward, leaving Theo behind in a haze of dust.

❧ Chapter Ten ❧

BALDWIN knew he should be paying attention to what the barons here in his tent were saying. After all, he had been the one who had called this council-of-war in the first place, and the things being argued were of utmost importance. But his thoughts kept drifting back to just how sick he was actually becoming, and he wondered which of these noblemen knew of it.

The secret had gotten out. Someone had told, and the awful truth was spreading through the camp like wildfire. Their King was a leper!

He felt so self-conscious sitting there in front of them all. Would they demand proof that the incredible story was nothing but a rumor? Would they make him take off his gloves, right here and now, so that they could see for themselves? His heart was racing at the very prospect of it, and he wished that he had let Theo come after all. God alone knew how hard it had been to leave him behind like that! And just now, Baldwin would give anything to have his best friend by his side.

But to his amazement, no one had yet mentioned his illness. No, they were discussing only Saladin and the difficulty of getting to Aleppo in time. The Count of Tripoli was saying something, and the others were becoming angry. Baldwin forced himself, with a huge effort, to stop thinking about all those ugly sores hidden beneath his mailshirt and to concentrate instead on their words.

"The city is already as good as lost," Tripoli was insisting. "We're just wasting our time out here, and if we had any sense at all we would—"

"You're only surmising, my lord!" interrupted Sir Gerard de Ridford. "We have no evidence of the conditions in Aleppo! If we turn back now, Saladin is assured of the victory. Yet if we continue, there is always the chance, however slim, that we can hold on to something."

"Slim is an understatement! Our troops will be exhausted by the time we even get there. We cannot possibly fight off the Sultan's entire army after such a journey. I say it's madness to continue!"

"So instead we should hand the territory to Saladin on a silver platter? Is that what you're suggesting?"

Tripoli glared first at Gerard de Ridford, then at the other barons surrounding him. "I am suggesting no such thing! I am merely looking at the facts and taking a realistic view."

"We have no facts!" De Ridford replied. "Certainly not enough to call off this whole endeavor."

"My lords," Sir Odo de Saint-Amand interrupted calmly, speaking for the first time; "before we engage further in this debate, I think we should listen to what His Majesty the King has to say." He pierced them all with a look, and the gathering of men reluctantly fell silent. "Sire?" Sir Odo continued. "I believe you've given this situation some thought over the past several hours?"

Baldwin felt his cheeks redden as all those pairs of eyes turned toward him. Instinctively he tucked his hands beneath the material of his surcoat and clenched them tightly together. He was nervous. Would they even listen to him? Would all these experienced knights care what a thirteen-year-old boy had to say?

He cleared his throat and began. "First of all, my lords, I want to thank you for agreeing to this meeting at such a late hour. I know these last few days have been long and you must all be very tired, but I—"

Sir Gerard de Ridford heaved an exaggerated sigh and cut in. "We're perfectly aware of our personal afflictions, Sire. If you would get to the point."

Baldwin felt a knot form in his stomach. No one would have dared to speak to his father like that!

He wished the Marshal hadn't come in here with Sir Odo. But, of course, it would have been impossible to hold this meeting without him. Sir Gerard might be a corrupt monk, but he was still the supreme military commander of the Templars, and as such his experience was invaluable.

Sir Odo shot the other Templar a look, but it went unheeded.

Baldwin tried to ignore the comment and made himself go on. "I tend to agree with my cousin, the Count of Tripoli," he said. "Aleppo is too far away and we'll never get there in time to do any good."

He saw Tripoli cast a satisfied smirk in De Ridford's direction. The Templar, in turn, bristled. Baldwin knew the two of them hated each other. They had been locked in a personal feud for years now and refused to agree on absolutely anything.

But the young King wasn't finished yet, and he sensed that the smugness would soon disappear from Tripoli's face the moment he went on.

He was right. It did. "I do not suggest, however, that we turn back to Jerusalem," Baldwin continued. "I have another plan. I think we should march this army to Damascus and attack there instead."

There was a stunned silence. All the barons simply

stared at him, disbelieving. For a moment Baldwin felt like crawling under his seat.

Then, to his relief, Sir Odo broke the silence. "Perhaps, Sire," he said respectfully, "you would care to explain your reasoning for such an unexpected proposal?"

Baldwin took a deep breath and tried to sit up a bit straighter. "It's quite simple, really," he replied. "Damascus is Saladin's capital city, right?"

"Of course, Sire," Tripoli said between clenched teeth. "We all know that!"

"Well, if he has taken his army to Aleppo, then Damascus must be left with only a small garrison to guard it. If we attack there, Saladin will be forced to raise the siege and bring his men back to defend his own city."

Again, the tent was plunged into silence.

Finally one of the barons spoke. "You're proposing a counterattack, Sire?" he asked.

"Yes. Give Saladin a choice. Aleppo or Damascus. He can have one, but not both." Baldwin held his breath for their reaction.

The noblemen exchanged cautious glances, trying to read each other's faces. Slowly a few murmurs and quiet comments rippled through the tent. And then, unexpectedly, Renaud de Chatillon, the Hawk of Kerak, let out a guffaw of pure delight and slapped his knee. "Brilliant!" he bellowed. "What an astute idea!" He looked around him and asked, "So, why didn't any of you masterminds think of it?"

Encouraged by his enthusiasm, a few others started to nod; agreement was heard from several voices. Sir Odo de Saint-Amand gave the King a look of open admiration and said, "Very well thought out, Sire. I think it's an excellent proposal."

"And I," snarled the Count of Tripoli, "think it's absurd!"

Everyone turned to look at him. "We are simpletons," he fumed, "if we actually think Saladin would leave Damascus as vulnerable as all that! Surely a third of his army, at the very least, will have been left there to defend—"

"If a third of his army has remained behind," Sir Gerard interrupted, "then Aleppo cannot be in that much danger. Make up your mind, my lord Tripoli. You can't have it both ways."

The heat rose to Tripoli's face and he stiffened. But he couldn't think of anything to say.

Baldwin studied the rest of the men for signs of opposition, but no one else seemed to object. As a matter of fact, their expressions showed that they were clearly in agreement. He couldn't believe it. They had actually listened to him! And even more astounding, not a single man had mentioned the rumors which were sweeping so quickly through the ranks. Baldwin felt a wave of relief wash over him. He stood up and said conclusively, "My lords, I think we should all try to get some sleep. Tomorrow at dawn we can change our course to Damascus, and with the help of God, this plan just might work. . . ."

∞ Chapter Eleven ∞

THE more he thought about it, the more depressed Tripoli became. He still couldn't believe it, couldn't believe that Saladin had raised the siege on Aleppo like that.

All the soldiers surrounding him were in high spirits, laughing and swaying in their saddles as if drunk with victory. Tripoli steered his horse to the side, away from them all, and glared at the King's mount far ahead of him.

This was a disaster! An irreparable disaster! That disease-ridden child had actually managed to scare off the Sultan's army! He had sent them racing back to Damascus like a bunch of terrified rabbits, and what was worse, he had won tremendous respect from his own thousands of knights in the process.

Tripoli couldn't figure out how the bold and hastily prepared attack had met with such astounding success, but it had. And Baldwin had just proved that he had the makings of a military genius. Nothing could possibly be worse!

"Plans gone astray, my lord?" a voice suddenly asked beside him.

He didn't need to turn his head to know who the speaker was. He could already see the splash of red cloth on white as the second horse appeared at his flank. "Shut up, De Ridford," he snapped. "Or has Sir Odo dispensed you from your sanctimonious silence of the march?"

The Templar Marshal laughed. "My, my, we are in a foul mood today. Not that easy to kiss your little dreams good-bye, is it?"

Tripoli kept his gaze straight ahead. "I have absolutely no idea what you're talking about."

"Come now, my lord Count. We all have our ambitions. Yours just happen to be more brazen than most."

Tripoli shot him a look. How much did Gerard de Ridford actually know? Surely he couldn't have guessed that he and Saladin were working together? He thought it wise, nonetheless, to change the direction of the conversation. Throw it back in De Ridford's face instead.

"Hah!" Tripoli scoffed. "You're the one to preach about brazen ambition, monk! It must have taken such untiring zeal and devotion on your part to rig that last election without poor Odo catching on."

To his disappointment, De Ridford didn't even try to deny it. If anything, he looked amused. It was common knowledge amongst the barons that he had swung those votes by immoral means, and all he said now was, "My position as Military Marshal of the Templars is in the best interests of the realm, I assure you."

"Naturally. Who wouldn't claim honorable motives when he has unrestrained command of the most powerful fighting force in all of Palestine?"

De Ridford shrugged casually. "I serve only Holy Mother Church."

"You serve only yourself!"

"And you, my lord? Whom do you serve?"

From behind them came a laugh. "Tripoli, I strongly suspect, serves Saladin," the Hawk of Kerak shot out. "Or was it just my imagination back there that he wanted Aleppo taken by the enemy?"

Tripoli felt his heart rate quicken.

Kerak rode up on the other side of him, grinning broadly, and gave him a rough slap on the shoulder. "I'm afraid, my friend, that whatever little support you had managed to retain among the nobles has just been jerked out from under your backside. And by a leper, at that! Ouch! Perhaps next time you'll think to put a cushion beneath you."

Tripoli had plenty of cushions, all right! There were other ways to get rid of the King, which had nothing to do with popular opinion. Prudently, he kept his mouth shut and said nothing.

"Oh, excuse me," Kerak continued, noting the Count's stony silence, "I see I've interrupted one of your loving parleys with Gerard. Tell me, which of you was it this time who showered the other with the biggest bouquet of roses?"

De Ridford smiled. "Poor Tripoli isn't in the chirpiest of moods right now, Kerak. Perhaps we'd best just leave him to lick his wounds alone."

"Say what you will," snapped Tripoli, trying to salvage some dignity, "but I'm looking out for all of our necks. Unless we can come to peaceful terms with Saladin soon, this Kingdom is on its last leg!"

"Peaceful terms!" the Templar scoffed. "Hear that, Hawk? He talks of peace with the Infidel! I wonder how many fiefdoms Saladin has promised him if he can achieve that!"

Tripoli gave a start. De Ridford had guessed!

The Hawk let out a laugh and, ignoring Tripoli's presence between them, answered De Ridford. "Well, he shall first have to think of a way to eliminate young Baldwin, shan't he?"

"I'd like to see him try."

"Ah, but he *has* been trying. Or have his efforts been so pathetic that you hadn't noticed?"

It was De Ridford's turn to laugh. "Now if I wanted power as bad as Tripoli does, I'd—"

"Don't you?" Kerak asked.

The Templar ignored the interruption and continued, "—I'd go about securing it in a much more rewarding way. I'd simply marry the heiress to the Throne, Her lovely Highness, the Princess Sibyl. If rumors are true, her brother won't be keeping his crown for long."

"Ah, you forget, my dear Gerard. She must wed him whom the King chooses and no other. Come now, surely an expert schemer like yourself can think of something better than that!"

Tripoli had had enough. He angrily spurred his horse forward and out of their company. He didn't need to listen to both a hawk and a fox stalking their prey.

✐ Chapter Twelve ✐

IT SEEMED to Theo as if his turn would never come. He had been milling around in this noisy, chattering crowd with a polite smile plastered on his face for what felt like hours. Usually he could get into the spirit of such festive celebrations as this, but today he had no interest whatsoever in the lively music of the minstrels or the platters laden high with the kitchen's choicest delicacies.

No, all he wanted was to see Dwin again.

He skirted his way past a group of wise-cracking young knights and the silly giggling maidens surrounding them, vying for their attention, and moved up closer to the front of the room. He knew they'd have only a minute or two together at the very most. There were far too many important people here today, far too many congratulations and stilted little speeches being thrust upon the victorious King right now. But even still, a couple of minutes together after so many long months apart was better than nothing at all.

Somehow he managed to wedge between two fat barons and finally reached the dais. King Baldwin was there, his head turned away in conversation with his uncle, the Senechal of Jerusalem. Well, Jocelin de Courtenay didn't seem such an old stick that he would resent a little interruption. Theo took his chances, moved forward, and bowed respectfully before the throne.

Thankfully, the Senechal indulged him and stopped speaking. Baldwin turned to look at the newcomer, and when he saw that it was his friend, his face lit up at once. "Theo!" he exclaimed.

Theo raised himself up, equally delighted. But when he looked at the King, a shock ran through him and he froze.

"Theo, I've missed you so much! There are so many things to tell you, you'll never believe it all!"

Theo blinked and struggled to regain his composure before poor Dwin would notice that anything was wrong.

His neck!

The high collar couldn't quite hide those patches of rotting skin along the left side of his throat. The disease was spreading, and it looked horrible! Yet Theo suspected Baldwin didn't even know. Should he tell him, or would that only make things worse? He wasn't sure what to do.

He felt Jocelin de Courtenay give him a stern nudge, and he remembered what he'd been instructed to say. Dropping to one knee in a reflex action, he kissed his friend's gloved hand. "Sire," he recited automatically, "welcome home. Allow me to congratulate you on such a fine victory."

Baldwin moaned. "Oh no, not from you as well! What on earth have they been teaching you while I've been gone?"

Theo couldn't help it. He had to laugh. He rose to his feet and forced himself to ignore those awful lumps. He'd let his friend know later, in private. After all, there was nothing Baldwin could do about it now anyhow, and to bring it up would only destroy his self-confidence for the next few hours. Obviously everyone else was ignoring it as well. Instead, Theo said, "You did it, Dwin! You actually beat the Sultan! The whole Kingdom is proud of you!"

The younger boy flushed at the praise. "It wasn't just me, Theo. It was all of them. I never knew how many brave knights God has given me in this realm."

Theo smiled, and everything felt back to normal. "Tell me," he asked mischievously, "is it true that Saladin has six eyes and horns on his head?"

Baldwin laughed. "I honestly wouldn't know. All I saw of him was his tail between his legs as he scampered back to those orange groves of Damascus."

"Well, you better believe he won't dare set another paw inside your kingdom again for a long—"

Before Theo had time to finish his sentence, someone elbowed him aside, and he saw Sir Humphrey de Toron give an elegant sweeping bow toward the throne.

"Sire," he gushed with obvious insincerity, "welcome home! Allow me to congratulate you on such a magnificent victory!"

Jocelin de Courtenay was immediately at Theo's side, ushering him out of the young earl's way and back into the crowd of unimportant nobodies.

And that, Theo was starting to suspect, was exactly the place where he was destined always to remain.

∾ Chapter Thirteen ∾

(1177, Three and a half years later)

SIR Odo de Saint-Amand tried hard to imagine what it must have been like when the air of the Temple had been pure and holy. For there was no denying that the grassy enclosure wherein he stood was, indeed, hallowed ground. Built upon the very site of Solomon's Temple—that glorious structure of ancient biblical times, so long ago destroyed—and thus deriving its name, the Templar monastery was separated from the Royal Palace by nothing more than a courtyard. Yet the Grand Master could remember, with sad nostalgia, how complete that separation once had been: world, pomp and pleasure on one side; penance, prayer and austerity on the other. Alas! If only such were still true!

Sir Odo knelt down on the damp ground and brushed away the patch of moss from the headstone before him, whispering a *Requiem aeternam* as he did so. There was no name chipped into the rock, but all the Templars knew whose bones lay beneath this spot. Hugh de Payns, their venerable founder. He, along with seven other zealous young noblemen, had been the humble beginnings of the Order. *The Poor Knights of Christ* was what he'd called his first little group of monks; it was only later, after King Baldwin the Second had granted them the abandoned Temple grounds, that their name had been changed. And, incredibly, in less than seventy

51

short years the Order had grown into the wealthiest and most influential military machine in the entire Catholic Church. There were now Templar chapters throughout the Holy Land, and countless novitiates in Europe as well.

But was it really the blessing of Almighty God, Sir Odo wondered sadly, which had caused the Order to flourish so quickly? Or was it rather the lust for honor and the unbridled urge to shed blood which drew so many young knights to enter the Templar monasteries? He would never know, of course. That was for God alone to decide, and it would all come out on Judgment Day. But Sir Odo couldn't help but long for a time when the corruption in the Order might miraculously be rooted out and Hugh de Payns would be able to look down and once again be proud of those who had followed in his footsteps.

The Grand Master crossed himself and closed his eyes for a quiet moment of prayer. But he had hardly had time for a single *Pater Noster* before he became aware of the presence of another. He looked up.

Well, speak of corruption. There stood Sir Gerard de Ridford himself.

Odo reluctantly rose from his knees and dusted the dirt from his habit. "Yes, Brother Marshal? What is it?"

"Forgive me for interrupting your devotions, my lord. There's someone at the gate who wishes to see you." De Ridford frowned. "It's the King's devoted lap dog, that Norman-bred Theodore de Thierceville."

The Master cocked an eyebrow. "*Sir* Theodore de Thierceville," he corrected. "He's knighted now, you know. Or hadn't you heard?"

"Oh yes, I've heard," De Ridford replied, disgusted. "Next His Majesty will be dubbing them in the cradle! I swear, the boy can't possibly be older than seventeen.

At least the whelp had enough brains to make friends in the right places."

Sir Odo felt the heat rise to his face. "You'll not speak dishonorably of this knight in my presence, Brother Gerard! He's had to earn the dignity in exactly the same manner as they all do! Besides," he added, "it wasn't even the King who dubbed him. His Majesty has been away, campaigning in the North, for well nigh two years now. He knows absolutely nothing about it."

"Then some baron made a mistake."

The Master of the Temple let out a laugh. "I doubt you would maintain that point of view for long, Brother, if you could see Sir Theodore's skill with a lance. Rumors run rampant that at last month's tournament he actually unhorsed three of Kerak's champions in the first charge." He chuckled to himself. "Oh, what I would have given to have seen the Hawk's face then!"

Well, even De Ridford had to smile at that. "Impressive," he admitted. "But unfortunately, my lord, tournaments have little to do with real warfare."

"Nor does attacking a pole with a blunted sword for an hour every day. Yet our Templars must do it anyhow. Now go, and bring me my visitor."

De Ridford inclined his head and turned to leave.

Sir Odo, on impulse, called him back. "Brother Gerard?"

The Marshal stopped. "Yes, my lord?"

"I daresay this realm would be a far holier place if we were all as sincerely devoted to the King's cause as this young Sir Theodore. Inside that diseased body of Baldwin the Fourth beats the valiant heart of a true Crusader, which every one of us would do well to imitate. Just try to remember that, will you?"

De Ridford coughed. "Why of course, my lord. I shall meditate upon it daily."

The Master watched him depart and felt his blood boil. He had to do something about all this filth! The Templars were his Order now, and it was his job to mop up the mess. But how? Things had been let go for far too long already. If he expelled De Ridford, he would have not only a rebellion, but possibly even a full-scale civil war on his hands. One couldn't just take the most formidable army in the entire Holy Land and split it in half without expecting an awful lot of blood to be spilled—and not just a few souls to be damned in the process.

No, he had to maintain peace. At least among his own monks. There were already enough outside enemies waiting to devour Christendom in their jaws.

The Master sighed heavily and tried to draw his thoughts instead to the King's young friend who would be here any moment. The visit came as no surprise, of course. He had known for years that as soon as the boy was knighted he would come knocking at the Jerusalem Temple, humbly begging for admission.

And he had equally known what his own answer would have to be. Not that he thought Theodore would make a poor Templar. Quite the contrary! The lad, like his father Sir Robert, had that fierce fighting blood in his veins which was so characteristic of the Norman race, yet it was tempered by true personal virtue. That, Sir Odo knew, was exactly the kind of knight Hugh de Payns would have been proud to number amongst his sons. Yet, unfortunately, there were other things to be considered as well. . . .

Once again, the Master of the Temple let out a sigh. Why was it, he wondered, that the harshest blows must always be dealt to those who least deserved them? He closed his eyes and whispered a prayer that God would grant the young knight the grace to accept this cross, and that someday he might even understand that it had been laid upon him only for his own good.

⨯ Chapter Fourteen ⨯

"**I** DON'T see why widows have to wear black all the time," Princess Sibyl griped. "It makes me feel like a prudish old bag and I'm sick of it!"

Lady Stephanie, the wife of Kerak, only laughed. "Oh, Sib," she said, "don't pout so much. Any man can see you're the same fresh daisy you were before your brother made you marry Sir William Longsword. Now hold still so I can adjust your coif. It's gone all lopsided."

Sibyl set her face in a sullen frown but obediently stopped squirming.

The older lady continued. "Besides, it won't be for too much longer. Your period of mourning is just about up, you know."

"My period of mourning was up the day they dumped William's corpse in the ground. It was a relief to be rid of the coot and it'll be an equal relief to shed this ugly witch costume."

Stephanie resumed dabbing on her own cosmetics. She never trusted her maids with the job of hiding those few little wrinkles. "Now, now," she chided, "don't be so impatient. The minute you become available again the King will only dig up another pious bore for you to marry, and chances are he'll be even worse than your first husband. So enjoy your freedom while you can, black dress and all."

Well, Stephanie should know. She'd been widowed twice. Sibyl merely shrugged and cast another resentful

55

glance toward the cradle at the far side of the room. She wished her son would wake up so that she could get his feeding over with. He was holding her back from the royal banquet in honor of the King's homecoming.

"Better watch it, Sib," Stephanie went on in a sudden burst of amusement. "I wouldn't be surprised if your brother chose that landless Norman he always used to hang around with. You know the one I mean. Sir Robert's son."

Sibyl jerked her eyes back to her cousin. "Theo?" she exclaimed. "Never! Baldwin wouldn't dream of it!"

"Why not? He fits the bill perfectly. Pure enough bloodlines, even if he has no estates to prove it."

Sibyl had never even thought of the possibility before. Now she did, long and hard. Hmm, he was pious, yes, but definitely not boring! Handsome as they came, too, and supremely chivalrous. She remembered that he had once offered to kill a rat for her when he had been nothing but a page in her father's household. After that she had been madly in love with him for at least an entire year.

"I wouldn't mind marrying Theo," she admitted to Stephanie at last. "Unfortunately, though, there are two things wrong with him."

"Only two?" Stephanie raised an eyebrow, impressed. "Well, I've never heard you say that about any other man! And what, pray tell, are these two glaring faults?"

"For one thing, I could never boss him around. And that's the main quality I want in a husband. When I'm Queen—and I will be someday—then I need a king at my side whom I can wipe my feet on. I'm going to rule this Kingdom my own way!"

"And this Theo fellow wouldn't be like that?"

"Are you joking? Bend to a woman! He'd rather die."

The Lady of Kerak smiled. "Sounds so much like my

own dear Hawk. And . . . his second unforgivable sin?"

Sibyl frowned, disappointed despite herself. "Theo left Jerusalem a couple months ago, shortly after he was knighted. No one knows where he went. If you ask me, he just couldn't bear the thought of our charming little leper latching onto him again, and who could possibly blame him for that?"

Stephanie arose, her face finished. "Well, that rather puts the stopper on the idea of marrying him, doesn't it?" She glanced at the cradle. "Isn't that baby of yours awake yet?"

"No." The Princess strode across the room and looked down at him, Prince Baldwin. Even the name she despised! Well, maybe she could give him to her mother to raise. Lady Agnes had a surprising maternal streak where her infant grandson was concerned, which suited Sibyl just fine. "Shall I wake him?" she asked. "I don't know about you, but I'm just dying to get downstairs and have a good close look at how sick my brother really is." She smiled maliciously. "Surely he can't live that much longer! And that bejeweled crown will look ever so much lovelier upon my head than upon his, don't you think?"

Lady Stephanie refrained from comment. Word had spread about how ghastly the poor King was starting to look; apparently a portion of his face, which had always promised to turn out so handsome, was now in shreds. She couldn't help but feel sorry for him. Baldwin was hardly seventeen years old, yet she had heard from her husband that he was a brilliant military commander and brave as the bravest of knights. He never used his humiliating illness as an excuse to shirk his duties, and Stephanie could only admire such courage.

She decided to change the subject back to Sibyl's sleeping baby. "Go ahead," she said, forcing a smile, "wake the little mite up. I'm sure the whole court is waiting for their Princess to arrive."

Sibyl reached into the cradle and lifted the tiny bundle into her arms. The baby jerked awake and let out a tired wail of protest.

"Typical male," Sibyl snarled. "Thinks of absolutely nothing but himself!"

ᵍᵉ Chapter Fifteen ᵍᵉ

(November, 1177)

THERE was no need to turn from the window and look in order for Baldwin to know exactly who had just entered the tower. He could instantly smell the perfumed handkerchief which Sibyl always held over her nose whenever she came anywhere near him. He knew she did it to embarrass him, of course, but even still he felt the shame. He stubbornly continued to gaze outside and pretended to ignore her.

"After all this time," she purred, "you're still watching for Theo to come riding back. I tell you, Baldwin, you're wasting your time. Why would he possibly want to see you again?"

The King wasn't in the mood to put up with her mockery just now. There were too many genuine worries on his mind. "I'm watching," he explained as kindly as he could, "for Tripoli's men. They should have been here ages ago."

"Tripoli, Tripoli. That's all I ever hear about is our cousin Tripoli! You never have trusted him, have you?"

Now Baldwin turned to face her. Poor Sibyl. She would be the Queen someday, yet she knew so little. "There are few men who can be trusted," he warned her, "and our cousin, sadly, is not one of them. Learn that now, my dear sister, and it'll save you a lot of trouble in years to come. Believe me."

As always happened when Baldwin tried to give her

gentle counsel, Sibyl refused to listen. She merely tossed her head, as if to say, *What do you know?* and accused, "You just think the good Count wants to get rid of you. That's all there is to it."

Everyone can see he's not the only one, Baldwin thought wryly, but he kept his mouth shut. There were so many things he longed to teach his sister—as their father had so carefully taught him—but Baldwin had learned by now that it was a waste of breath. All he could do was pray for Sibyl, which he did with all his heart, and hope that God would soon send another worthy nobleman to become her new husband and thus the future king.

Baldwin resumed staring out the window, scanning every inch of the horizon for a sign of Tripoli's heralds. They were meant to have vital information on Saladin's whereabouts. The Sultan, like Theo, had seemingly vanished off the face of the earth, and Christians were living in a state of continual apprehension. It was disconcerting, to say the least, when the enemy simply disappeared!

"If you ask me," Sibyl volunteered sweetly, "he's gone back to Normandy, where his parents were born."

"Saladin's parents weren't born in Normandy, I can assure you."

"Not him, dummy. Theo, I mean."

Baldwin, naturally, had known exactly whom she meant. He didn't deign to reply.

"You were gone for two whole years, you know. That was plenty of time for poor Theo to come to his senses and decide he didn't really want to decompose into some kind of ugly ghoul as well. Can you blame him?"

Despite himself, Baldwin flinched. He realized, too late, that that was exactly the reaction his sister had hoped for. "If Theo has gone to Normandy," he told her steadily, "then he had his own good reasons, and I wish him nothing but God's blessings."

He suspected that Sibyl was about to say something else, no doubt to goad him on, but fortunately she didn't get the chance. Just then a group of horsemen appeared over a rise far below.

There was no mistaking the emblem on their surcoats. Tripoli's men.

The King spun around and quickly left the tower, eager to hear the information they would bring. At least Saladin's mysterious whereabouts might be revealed to him, even if not those of the friend whom he loved as a brother and missed more than he was ever willing to admit.

∽ Chapter Sixteen ∾

BROTHER Bernard Labouisse of the Gaza Chapter of Templars leaned forward in his saddle, straining to get a better view from his post on the summit of the hill. The heat rippled the air around him like a watery veil, and his eyes were already stinging from the dust.

"Hey, Brother Marcel," he beckoned to the knight a few yards away. "Do you see that thing down there? Or am I just imagining it?"

Brother Marcel Jourdanne moved his horse closer and lifted a hand to shield his eyes against the blinding glare of the sun. "I don't see anything."

"Way in the distance. Something's moving, I'm sure of it."

For a moment the other Templar said nothing, but Bernard knew he had spotted it as well. A churning brown haze on the edge of the horizon. The two young knights simply stared, trying to figure out what it might be.

"What do you make of it?" Bernard asked.

Marcel didn't answer, but twisted in his saddle and gave a shout. "Brother Geoffrey! Come up here! There's something you'd better have a look at."

The leader of their patrol, Sir Geoffrey Chateauneuf, was not much older than they, but he knew the desert better than anyone. He spurred his horse forward and trotted to the summit of the hill, and the three remaining knights in their patrol followed. "What's wrong?" he asked.

"I think we've got some kind of a sandstorm blowing this way."

Geoffrey followed with his gaze as his brother pointed to the south, out there in the direction of Egypt. Then he too leaned forward and shaded his eyes.

He drew in a sharp breath. "Dear God!" he gasped. "That's no storm!"

Brother Bernard felt the hairs on the nape of his neck prickle. "Then what is it?"

"You don't know?"

"No."

Geoffrey turned to him. "That's an army on the march," he said. "And believe me, it must be enormous!" The other five Templars exchanged startled glances, then the confusion in their eyes quickly gave way to horror.

"They're heading this way, straight toward Jerusalem!" Marcel blurted out. "And we're the only thing out here blocking their path!"

Geoffrey felt his heart start to pound. Marcel was right. There wasn't a single Christian army to stop them for at least two hundred miles! Nearly every knight in the Kingdom, including part of their own Gaza Chapter, had ridden north weeks ago, where some high-ranking Count had assured His Majesty that the Sultan would attack.

"We've never been invaded from Egypt!" another Templar exclaimed. "What's going on?"

Geoffrey fought down the panic swelling up inside him. "Looks like someone betrayed the King. That has to be Saladin out there! No one else has that much manpower."

"But Jerusalem is ungarrisoned!" Bernard gasped. "She's entirely defenseless!"

"Where's the King?" someone demanded.

Geoffrey tried hard to think. "He's still in the city. At least he was the last I heard. He was too sick to travel north with his troops."

"Then somehow we've got to warn him!"

Geoffrey realized that, of one accord, all of his brothers had turned their eyes to him for guidance. He was the senior knight here, the one who had been in the Order the longest. It had only been for ten years, but considering the number of battles he had fought, that was a respectable lifespan.

Geoffrey knew he had to keep calm. "We have no time to waste," he told the others. "We need to get back to Gaza and let the rest of our brothers there know what's happening."

"But there are only thirty of us! We can't stop an entire army!"

Geoffrey drew in a deep breath and returned his gaze to the horizon. Yes, that was Saladin out there all right. And every one of his instincts was screaming at him to move, and quickly!

"All right, listen," Geoffrey began. "This is what we'll do. Brothers Bernard and Marcel, you're coming with me. We're off to Jerusalem to alert the King. If we ride all night we just might get there in time. The rest of you, get back to Gaza, and don't stop for lunch on the way!"

"Then what?" someone asked.

Geoffrey had no idea. He wasn't cut out to make decisions of this magnitude! The survival of the Christian Kingdom was hanging on whatever instructions he gave these other Templars, and he had to say the right thing.

He breathed a quick prayer, begging God for guidance. Then he ordered, "Get our brothers and slip out along the coast. Meet us at Ascalon. You know the place I mean? It's southwest of Jerusalem."

One of them nodded. "I know it. There's a plain there, and a dry river bed."

"Right. That's the place. If we have to fight, then that's the spot I'd choose to do it. I think the King would agree."

"We don't stand a chance!" Brother Bernard exclaimed. "We're history, every single one of us! The Kingdom of Jerusalem is lost!"

Geoffrey knew it was true. King Baldwin could never gather together any sizable force at such short notice. But even so, they had to warn him. "We'll do the best we can," Geoffrey replied. "So let's get moving!" He wheeled his horse around and spurred it savagely in the flanks. It bolted, taking off at a dead gallop across the desert.

The others exchanged desperate looks, then split into two groups and literally rode for their lives.

❧ Chapter Seventeen ❧

THERE were so many of them! Just so many Saracens, right there on the plain of Ascalon directly below, less than a mile distant. Baldwin had never seen such a fearsome sight, and it was with an effort that he tore his gaze away and looked instead at the Templar mounted beside him.

He tried to remember the man's name. Geoffrey, yes, that was it. Sir Geoffrey Chateauneuf. Baldwin knew instinctively that this was a knight he could trust. He had sensed that straight away, from the very minute Geoffrey and his two brothers from Gaza had come flying through the gates of Jerusalem as if the devil himself had been at their heels. The trio had arrived almost on the point of collapse, so hard had they ridden throughout the entire night, yet even then they had thought of nothing but the salvation of the Kingdom.

"We have to stop them," Baldwin said now. "I'm not sure how, but I won't let them take Jerusalem."

"Sire, Saladin must have at least thirty thousand men down there. Possibly more."

Baldwin had arrived at that same ominous calculation. He said nothing. His eyes traveled from Brother Geoffrey to the tiny gathering of men behind them, hardly more than three hundred in number. Not all were even soldiers; some were merely old men or young squires who had bravely taken up what arms they could and volunteered to fight. Under such dire circumstances, Baldwin had hardly been able to refuse. He watched them now, scrambling to get themselves into some kind of respectable order, with no real leaders among them. Which of the two armies it was harder to look at, the young King couldn't quite decide—the infernal enemy on the plain, or his own few gallant and loyal Crusaders, so many of whom he feared would die this day.

"What orders," Sir Geoffrey asked respectfully, "shall I give my brethren?"

Baldwin knew he had to make a decision. But what?

If only someone with real experience were here! Someone like Master Odo de Saint-Amand, or Sir Gerard de Ridford. Even the incorrigible Hawk of Kerak would be welcome at his side just now!

But there was no one. No one here whom Baldwin could turn to for guidance. They were all up north, hundreds of miles away, where he himself had so foolishly sent them!

No, it was just himself and this scruffy band of well-meaning volunteers. Thirty were Templars, yes—but what could so few of them possibly do?

"Sire," Sir Geoffrey ventured, "if I may offer an opinion?"

"Yes, Brother Templar. Please do."

"The Sultan's army does not seem very disciplined just now. Look at the way they're trying to cross that dry river bed. They're not having an easy time of it, and at that rate it could take them days to get so many men over to this side. We still have a little bit of time."

Time. Perhaps. But of what use was time?

Baldwin studied the enemy's position carefully. It was true, there was little order down there. Horses and camels were balking at the deep plunge into the dry riverway; pack animals were scrambling for footholds all along the banks. The clay was crumbling beneath their hooves, men were stuck in the ditches and spreading farther and farther apart in a vain search for an easier passage. Absolutely none of their divisions was in battle formation of any kind.

They were, in fact, in total chaos.

The Muslims, however, didn't appear particularly worried about their lack of organization. No, they were perfectly smug in the knowledge that this tiny group of Christians watching them from the hilltop could never stop them, would never dare come a single step closer. Jerusalem was theirs for the taking; they knew it, and they were in no hurry.

Baldwin drew in a deep breath. "What do you think?" he asked. "If we made a charge, right now, this very minute, would they have time to pull themselves together and repel us?"

Brother Geoffrey stiffened in his saddle and let out a low whistle. Baldwin could imagine exactly what he must be thinking. *Suicide!* But the knight based his answer on experience rather than on personal sentiment. "That's the last thing in the world they would be expecting, Sire. One thing I can guarantee, we would catch them completely off guard."

"Armies have been known to panic at the unexpected. Am I right, Brother Templar?"

"Yes, Sire. I've seen it happen myself, more than once."

"So have I. Such a bold move might convince them that they've ridden straight into some kind of a deadly trap."

The knight said nothing. Baldwin suspected he was holding his breath. He felt his own pulse quicken. Could it work? *This was madness!*

Thirty thousand against a mere three hundred! What

on earth was he even thinking of?! But his Kingdom was at stake! God's Holy Kingdom was at stake!

"Let's do it!" he ordered. "Now. Before I have time to change my mind."

Sir Geoffrey stared at the King in disbelief. But the knight knew his place and would not dream of contradicting his Sovereign. Instead, all he said was, "Sire, who shall lead the charge?"

Baldwin didn't hesitate. "I will," he answered. This was his realm. God had entrusted it into his hands alone, and if it must fall, then it was going to fall over his own dead body.

"My brothers and I volunteer to ride in the vanguard, Sire, if you will grant us that honor."

Baldwin felt a wave of gratitude and relief wash over him. There might only be thirty Templars back there, but there was no one he would trust more to follow at his heels.

"Thank you," he said, knowing how insufficient were the words.

Sir Geoffrey spun his horse around and dug his spurred boots into the animal's sides. He set off at a lope toward the Christians waiting in the distance, and King Baldwin followed.

The Bishop of Bethlehem was there, mounted on a donkey, at the head of the hastily assembled troops. He had already granted the general absolution and was now holding, high above his head, the Standard of the Kingdom, with a relic of the True Cross in a bejeweled gold box upon a pole for all to see. The Prelate didn't need to ask what decision had been made; the moment he saw the two riders' faces, he knew. Crossing himself, he silently began to pray.

The King and the knight bowed their heads in reverence as they cantered past the holy relic, but didn't break their stride. They stopped only when they reached the little band of Gaza Templars, already fully armored and mounted in silence, some distance apart from the rest of the noisy, milling crowd of secular knights and infantry.

Sir Geoffrey merely gave his brethren a signal, no doubt informing them that they would make the first charge. None of the Templars protested. There wasn't a single movement among them. No, nothing but silent obedience.

The King nudged his horse sideways and slowly rode along in front of the Templar line. They looked so unreal, these warrior monks, all perfectly immobile and exactly the same, with their long deadly lances loosely couched before them. But yes, they were real, all right. Baldwin could see none of their faces beneath their full helms, but the pairs of eyes behind each steel mask met his own, and he knew they must all be just as scared and uncertain as he. He could only hope they were unable to see his own apprehension.

He knew that, as their King, he should say something to them. He should make some valiant little speech which would inflame their hearts and calm their minds. It was his duty to impart the courage and reassurance they would all need, and certainly none of them would dare utter a word without his bidding. Yet he was keenly aware of the effect the sight of a leper could have upon others, and because of that he had always left it to Sir Odo, or the Master of the Hospitallers, to rouse the troops' fighting blood and inspire them before a battle.

Even apart from that, what could he possibly say to this brave group of men whom he was virtually sentencing to death?

If only there were but one person here who might help him!

Somewhere along the line a single black stallion broke rank and impatiently pranced forward a few paces. But its rider obediently pulled it back in among the others where it belonged.

No one else moved.

Brother Geoffrey Chateauneuf slipped into his own position to the left of the miscreant warhorse and put on his helm. He, too, was now but a faceless statue.

Baldwin knew he had to address them. It was the King's job to inspire his troops! Then, unexpectedly, one of those identical figures, hidden behind some helm of black steel, actually dared to speak first, actually tried to help out poor Baldwin.

"Sire," he said quietly, "God wills it."

The Battle Cry of the Crusaders. The three words which had filled them and their forefathers with courage in battle for nearly a hundred years.

The words had been soft, yet not only the King but also the Templar's brothers had heard them, and the hearts of thirty-one men beat just a little more bravely.

Before Baldwin had a chance to say anything, another monk was bold enough to echo his brother's sentence, only much louder. *"Deus le vult!"*

The familiar cry reached the ears of a few others beyond the Templar line and was instantly taken up by a dozen men scattered out there among the troops.

"Deus le vult! God wills it!"

They all heard it now, and conversation out there ceased. Baldwin felt a tingle run down his spine as a hush fell slowly upon his entire army. He knew what was coming next and he braced himself for it, his own heart swelling with new-found strength.

Then, like some great tidal wave, the shout rang out, rose higher and louder, until it was surging through the entire Christian force. Baldwin listened with pride and admiration as a chorus of three hundred voices began to chant at him, over and over again.

"God wills it, Sire! God wills it!"

"Deus le vult! Deus le vult!"

Even the horses now were fired, straining at the bits, and the knights had to use all their strength to hold them back from the charge.

The Bishop of Bethlehem appeared at the young King's side with the Standard of the Realm, and Baldwin raised his eyes to see the golden reliquary containing a fragment of the True Cross. This very same wood had once borne the dying Body of the Son of God.

Baldwin slid down from his saddle and knelt on the ground before that most blessed relic. Of himself, he could never lead this tiny handful of faithful Crusaders to so impossible a victory, but there was another King, to Whom all things were possible.

He could hear now that the shouting behind him was diminishing, replaced by a reverent hush, and he knew all eyes were watching him alone. These were true Crusaders, perfect knights all of them, no matter their birth or rank. They would pray with him; they would help him move Heaven to his aid!

Baldwin fell onto the dirt and prostrated himself in the form of a cross before the Holy Wood. "O Almighty God," he begged, "do not let Jerusalem fall! Take my life if Thou wilt, but please spare this holy Kingdom from the hands of the Infidel. And spare these men from the sword, they who are Thy true and faithful servants. Through Jesus Christ Thy Son Our Lord. Amen."

An audible gasp went up from the hundreds of soldiers behind, and even with his face pressed to the ground, Baldwin became aware of an immense, dazzling light somewhere high above him. It was so bright that for a moment he was blinded.

A sense of the supernatural gripped him, and, as if by some compelling force, he rose to his knees and looked up.

There in the sky, amidst a great flame of radiant light, was a majestic figure mounted upon a white stallion, and something deep inside whispered to Baldwin exactly who it was. Saint George, the heavenly Patron of Knighthood.

The vision vanished as quickly as it had appeared, and the sky returned to its normal cloudless blue.

There wasn't a sound or a movement in the whole Christian army. Nothing. Absolutely nothing. It was as if all present, man and beast alike, were transfixed by what they had just seen, unable to move.

But Baldwin knew they had a job to do.

Rising to his feet, he swung back into the saddle. Then, without even a glance behind, fully confident that the others would follow, he drove his spurs deep into his destrier's flanks and led the charge.

❦ Chapter Eighteen ❧

ALTHOUGH Brother Geoffrey had been through this many times before, he doubted he would ever grow used to the feeling of a charge. His whole body was burning with adrenaline and exaltation, strangely mixed with a sickening fear. He was packed so tightly between his two brothers that their legs and stirrups bumped against his; their shields would serve to guard him as well, and all thirty horses moved as one mighty and invincible phalanx of Templars stretching beyond him in both directions.

"Deus le vult!"

The shout was drowned out by the thunderous drumming of three hundred sets of hooves behind them, but Geoffrey knew it still rang out loud and true.

"God wills it! God wills it!"

The huge horses were rapidly gathering speed, lengthening their stride, and there was no stopping them now. They were flying, sailing over the earth, shortening the distance between themselves and the enemy at a frightful pace. Geoffrey knew the impact would come soon and he braced himself for it, couching his lance in front of him for the kill.

He kept his eyes fixed on the back of the King, directly ahead of him, and leaned lower in his saddle. It was a fight in itself to balance the long wooden pole in his grip and keep it stable. Reins and shield together in one hand, lance in the other. And hold the line!

A gap suddenly formed between himself and the skittish horse on his right as its rider no doubt struggled to position his weapon and hold it steady. But, difficult or not, they simply had to stay together!

Geoffrey steered his own galloping mount nearer and managed to close the gap. The entire wall on his left also shifted over.

Hold the line, Geoffrey silently begged. *Whatever you do, Brother, just hold this line!*

Though his vision was limited, he could now make out the Turks ahead of them, and he realized that the Christians had, indeed, caught them entirely unprepared. White-robed figures were flying in all directions, terrified men and animals bowling each other down in a frenzied and chaotic attempt to get out of the way of the knights' charge. Cries of panic rent the air as hands scrambled for shields and swords and axes.

"*Deus le vult!* God wills it!"

"God wills it!"

From somewhere to the left a shower of arrows darkened the sky and streamed down upon the Crusaders. Of one accord thirty wooden shields were raised, thirty brothers dodged beneath them. The entire rank of steel-clad Templars passed through the deadly rainfall unscathed. It would take a lot more than arrows to stop them!

"God wills it! God wills it!"

The Muslims directly ahead were running now in stark terror. Those who had armed themselves to brave the attack were quickly changing their minds, and there were no leaders among them to order otherwise. The whole Saracen army was disintegrating into a tangle of flapping robes, tripping camels and bolting steeds.

And then, the Crusaders slammed into them.

King Baldwin first, plunging headlong into their midst. Geoffrey caught a glimpse of him raising his sword before he was enveloped in the confusion and vanished.

A split second later he felt the shattering collision as his own heavyhorse and those of the unbroken wall of his brothers rode straight into Saladin's thirty thousand men.

His lance splintered and he dropped it. All around him were the splashing of blood and the grotesque sounds of crunching and screams as the Templars' huge warhorses trampled over whatever happened to be in their way. The sheer mass of bodies slowed them, but it could not stop them, and they just kept on going.

Geoffrey drew his sword and, along with his twenty-nine brothers, got down to the serious business of hacking through Saracen flesh and bone.

❧ Chapter Nineteen ❧

SIR Marcel Jourdanne saw the ax swinging down but was powerless to stop it. He flung his shield to the side to protect his brother from the blow, but his attempt was too late and in vain. A fountain of blood squirted into the air and another Templar went down.

He was the third.

The riderless horse bolted forward and disappeared among a hundred others, while Marcel steered over to close the gap. The monks always stayed together.

He had no idea how long they'd been at it, but the sun, now a flaming red ball in the sky, was a lot lower than it had been when this nightmare began.

The fighting was slowing down. Strength was fast ebbing for all concerned, thirst becoming intolerable, and the thick carpet of writhing bodies and dead animals strewn upon the slippery ground became harder and harder to move through.

But, incredibly, the Christian army still stood firm! All these hours later, and most of them remained alive! They were scattered now, fighting in little pockets for miles around, but Marcel knew that they would not be vanquished.

He couldn't understand it. So many thousands upon thousands of corpses in this vast desert plain, and nearly every one of them was a Turk.

It was a miracle. There was simply no other explanation.

Brother Marcel swung his sword at the next swarthy figure that suddenly loomed before him, and the two fell into the familiar rhythm of clashing steel.

Then, out of the corner of his eye, he saw the one thing he never dreamed he'd see. One of his brothers broke away from the fighting, savagely spurred his destrier forward and headed off alone at a gallop.

Marcel grimaced with disgust. He could not believe it.

One of his very own brothers had actually deserted the battle and fled.

Chapter Twenty

KING Baldwin knew now that God had truly accepted the offer he had made of his life. He was about to die, and his soul was ready.

No way could he hold out against this assault for much longer. The Saracen about to cut him down was one of the Sultan's own guards, a Mameluke, the absolute best of the best, and Baldwin knew it was all over. But God had been good to him, had let him first see this miraculous Christian victory before his soul would take flight; the young King could die knowing that his Realm would survive this day.

The Crown would pass to his sister Sibyl, but at least it would not go to Saladin. He could only pray that the man she chose to rule at her side would be a strong and worthy king, as true a Crusader as these few brave Christians who had fought at his side today. As for himself, Baldwin could meet his own Judgment knowing that he had kept all that had been entrusted to his care.

The motion of his heavy sword swaying back and forth at his opponent had become merely automatic; defeat was just a matter of time. But the human instinct for survival would not allow him to surrender, so he fought on. If he had been blessed with health and vigor, then maybe—just maybe—he might stand a chance. But his body of only seventeen years was already corroded with disease; he felt so weak and exhausted. With no sensation in his hands and arms, he had almost no control of his weapon.

His horse, receiving a mortal blow, collapsed beneath him into a crimson pool. Baldwin jumped clear of its thrashing hooves and managed to scramble back to his feet. But his sword was lost in the carnage and he could see two more swift Arabian ponies charging straight at him, the riders' gleaming scimitars already poised high above their heads. They knew, of course, by his golden surcoat emblazoned with the royal coat of arms that this was the King of Jerusalem, and to be the ones to spill his blood would be the greatest triumph of their lives.

Baldwin could hear their high ululating war cry as the two Mamelukes galloped headlong toward him to join their comrade for the kill, and his muscles went taut. He held his breath and waited helplessly for the onslaught.

Suddenly, from nowhere, an enormous black charger thundered in front of him and blocked the path of his three assassins. Baldwin stumbled back just in time to avoid the massive pawing legs as the stallion reared high into the air. Then its hooves slammed to the earth with a thud, and the King saw the flash of glistening steel as a sword was raised and came slashing ferociously down toward the Sultan's three startled guards.

There was no need to look for the emblem on the blood-splattered surcoat to know that this was a Templar, for no one but a Templar could fight like that! The knight hacked at the trio of Mamelukes with unimaginable fierceness, and the first fell, only to be crushed beneath that giant heavyhorse.

One down, two to go.

Baldwin dropped to his knees and fumbled to retrieve his own sword. Its hilt was slathered with blood, but he managed to grasp it nonetheless and sprang to help his rescuer.

Another Saracen was galloping toward them from the side, closing in with lightning speed. The King realized that he had to get out of the horse's line before the thing trampled him. His eyes darted about for an escape, but there was nowhere to run! He was trapped here, dead center in the flying beast's path.

He became aware of something, some vice-like pressure on his arm. He could discern it even despite his lack of feeling. He realized suddenly that the Templar, too, had seen the other horse coming, and was attempting with one hand to haul Baldwin onto his own charger whilst struggling to fight off the two Mamelukes at the same time. Baldwin frantically grabbed hold of him and scrambled into the saddle just as the third Turk went sailing past, leaning far over the side of his swift pony and slicing his scimitar into the space where Baldwin had stood just a second before.

But there was certainly no time to thank the Templar now. No, there was only time to fight! Mounted together, the King and his loyal subject fought off their two remaining attackers with all the strength they each had left, until both Mamelukes finally went down and the black charger was able to bolt clear of the carnage.

Everything was happening so quickly that Baldwin's mind was in a whirl. It was all he could do to hang on for dear life as the stallion raced across the desert plain toward safety. Then, just when he was sure he could hold on no longer, the Templar reined in, and gradually their mount straggled to an unsteady stop, its coat bathed in sweat and its sides heaving.

For a long moment neither rider could do a single thing other than sit there gasping to fill his lungs with air. Finally the Templar twisted around in the saddle. From beneath the steel helm his muffled voice managed to ask, "Sire, are you all right?"

Baldwin had no way of being certain whether or not he was wounded, but he breathlessly answered, "Yes, I think so."

The Templar studied him through the narrow eye slits of the helm, looking for fresh blood beneath all the filth. Then he pulled off his steel gauntlets and reached back. Carefully he ran his fingers along the dark crimson stain he had spotted on the shoulder of Baldwin's hauberk. He was searching for damaged links of chain, trying to assure himself that the blood there belonged to another, and that his King's mailcoat had not been sliced and the flesh torn open beneath. Baldwin was grateful for such solicitude.

After a moment, however, the Templar seemed satisfied. His King was dirty and exhausted, yes, but that was all. "I don't think you're wounded anywhere," he said.

"And what about you, Brother Templar?" Baldwin asked. "Are you hurt?"

"No, Sire."

"You saved my life. I can never pay the debt of gratitude I owe you."

"You owe me nothing. My loyalty and service belong to thee, Sire. I only thank God that you're unharmed."

With no other word, the knight turned around and urged their horse into a gentle lope across the battlefield.

The fighting was all over now; for as far as their burning eyes could see, there was nothing but slaughtered Turks littering the plain of Ascalon. Mile upon mile of blood-drenched corpses, and nearly every one of them an Infidel.

Little groups of survivors were banding together here and there, their tattered robes flapping in the evening breeze, but they were no threat now to Jerusalem. No, Saladin's great army of thirty thousand existed no more.

Baldwin knew the Sultan himself had just barely escaped upon a camel and had been pursued by a handful of Christians. But they had lost him in the end, and he was still alive out there somewhere. Yet it would be a long while before he could gather enough forces to strike God's Kingdom again.

The farther the two rode, the more Baldwin realized that the infinite power of God alone had wrought this. No victory so great could ever have been won by human hands.

The only thing which saddened him was the thought of so many souls having gone to perdition, and he prayed silently that a few Infidels, at least, may have somehow received Christian Faith and Baptism of Desire before going to meet their Eternal Judge.

At last the Templar halted on the summit of a rise, and for a long time the two riders just sat and gazed down at the valley below in silence and awe. The only sounds now were the flocks of vultures swooping down to finish the work of a thousand swords.

Then the knight quietly spoke. "It's a miracle, Dwin. By your prayers and the help of Saint George, we crushed Saladin's entire army."

"It wasn't my prayers alone, Brother Templar. God saw the purity of all these Crusaders. Every one of you helped to—" Baldwin suddenly stopped as his companion's words sank in. Only one person had ever called him by that name. He felt his heart miss a beat, and stared at the knight's back, stunned.

"*Theo?*" he whispered uncertainly. "Is . . . that you?"

The Templar turned to look at him, and that faceless steel helm merely nodded.

For at least a full half-minute Baldwin was speechless. Then he blurted out, "I never knew! I had no idea you were here!"

"I was right behind you, Sire. All the way."

"But . . . I don't understand! How did—"

"I was knighted before you came home. Sir Odo let me enter the Temple at Gaza."

Baldwin tried to take it in somehow, but it was just too much. So many emotions were already wrestling with each other after all these long hours of battle, and he was drained. It was all so overwhelming!

Then he spotted a group of horsemen approaching from the distance and realized that they were his squires. They were coming to get him and attend to his needs. "I've got to go find the rest of our army," he said. "Ride with me, Theo. Please. I want us to stay together."

Theo was quiet for so long that Baldwin started to wonder if he'd even heard. But at last his friend answered. "I broke rank with my brothers," he said sadly, "and by thy leave, Sire, I must return to them."

Baldwin felt his heart grow heavy. They'd been separated for nearly three years, and he missed Theo so badly! But then, he realized with a shock that this was the first time his friend had seen him since the disease had marred his face, and despite himself he cringed. He knew he looked awful.

"Theo," he said, "tell me the truth. Why did you leave Jerusalem? Was it to get away from me?"

Theo hesitated. "Yes," he finally admitted. "But it wasn't for the reason you're thinking, Dwin. Honestly. Master Odo commanded me to leave. I didn't choose to."

"Sir Odo made you leave? But . . . why? You could have entered the Temple there."

"He wouldn't let me. He told me that—" Theo paused, as if trying to remember the Master's exact words. After a moment he continued, "He told me that a heart attached to any creature, in no matter how pure or honorable a friendship, is still a heart divided for God. He said that if I truly wanted to serve you, my King, then I must first learn to love Our Lord alone. Only then could I be a perfect knight. He sent me away to Gaza so that I couldn't be near you."

Baldwin just stared at him, unable to think of anything to say. But there was no time anyway, for his squires reined in beside them.

Theo reached back to help his King dismount, and as Baldwin slid to the ground their hands met. Even through the thick material of his glove and the numbness of his dying skin, he was able to feel that firm and secure handclasp of friendship, and he understood then that they would never really be apart.

"God wills it, Sire," Theo said softly.

Baldwin realized then which Templar it had been who had first sounded that battle cry, the spark of which had spread so rapidly and inflamed the hearts of his Crusaders with such burning courage.

"*Deus le vult*, my most faithful knight," he whispered in reply.

Theo gave Baldwin's hand one more tight squeeze before reluctantly letting go. Then he spurred the black charger and galloped away alone across the darkening sands of Ascalon.

Chapter Twenty-One

A T long last, Princess Sibyl had found him. The perfect man. Young, handsome, debonair. Impeccable bloodlines.

And an absolute wimp.

She cupped her chin in her hands and smiled to herself as she watched him at the table across the crowded banquet hall. Fresh off the boat from France, he knew no one here, knew nothing of the politics or ways of Outremer. To manipulate him would be child's play.

He had already noticed her as well. How could he not, after all? Every man noticed the Princess of Jerusalem; she made absolutely certain of that! She waited patiently for him to catch her eye again. All evening he'd been stealing glances in her direction, doubtless thinking she wouldn't catch on. But how easy it was to guess exactly what was going on in that fair French head.

At last his eyes slid toward the high table once again, and Sibyl flashed him her sweetest smile. He, in return, smoothed back his hair with the palm of his hand and raised an eyebrow in rakish appraisal. The Princess modestly looked away.

If he wanted her, let him work for it! After all, she was going to make him a king someday.

Sibyl gracefully rose from her place at the table and swept her way over to her brother's side. A page scrambled to bring her a seat. She hated sitting so close to Baldwin; she would rather die than catch his revolting disease. But sometimes it just couldn't be helped. She even decided to dispense with her scented handkerchief.

"My dearest brother," she cooed, "I have just the teensiest little favor to ask you."

The King didn't fall for it. "Most likely the answer will be no," he said with a weary sigh, "but go ahead. Ask and get it over with."

He was tired and unwell tonight. She could tell straight away. Maybe this wouldn't be so hard after all. He didn't look like he was in the mood for a fight.

"That young nobleman sitting over there." She indicated with a movement of her eyes. "The one trapped between Sir Humphrey and the Hawk, poor thing."

The King glanced across the room. "Guy de Lusignan," he informed her.

She knew that already.

"He's new around here," Baldwin continued. "What about him?"

Sibyl shrugged innocently and sidled a little closer. "Oh, I don't know. He just looks so . . . lost. Forlorn. You know what I mean."

No reaction.

"I was thinking that maybe, well, it might be a token of kindness, an act of good will, if you were to give him some appointment at court. Make him feel a bit welcome."

The King smiled, amused. "I've already made him feel welcome. He's sitting here, isn't he?"

This wasn't working very well. Sibyl tried again. "Don't get me wrong. Not an important office or anything. Perhaps just a minor—"

"No. Not a hope."

Sibyl bristled, but kept the smile arranged on her face.

"Why not?"

No one was listening, but the King lowered his voice anyhow. "The positions in my court are already filled to my satisfaction. I don't need his type cluttering up this palace on a permanent basis."

So, Baldwin had been doing his own private investigations on Guy de Lusignan as well.

"Mother likes him."

"Mother would." Baldwin took a sip of his wine, then turned to look at his sister. "What you don't seem to realize, Sibyl," he said quietly, "is that while you're trying so hard to manipulate me all the time, others are planning to use you as a pawn in their own games as well. And, as much as we love our own mother, I hate to say that she's among them."

The Princess bit her lip. "I'm not trying to manipulate anyone! I'm simply trying to help out the poor—"

"Well, that's a first."

Sibyl clenched her teeth and struggled to hold her temper in check. "You know nothing about Sir Guy!"

"And you do?" Baldwin gave her no chance to answer, but continued, "I know enough about him, Sibyl, to promise you right now that he'll never sit upon my Throne. So just forget it."

She couldn't help it. She flared. How did he always guess her game?!

"You can't stop me, Baldwin!" she blurted out, a bit too loudly. "You have absolutely no power whatsoever—"

But before she had time to finish her sentence, her brother pushed back his chair and rose to his feet. Instantly a hundred other seats were vacated as well and all conversation ceased. A respectful hush fell over the entire room.

The King of Jerusalem smiled down at his sister,

accepted his royal robe from his attendants and majestically took his leave amidst a sea of bending backs.

⁓ Chapter Twenty-Two ⁓

"**I**T would be most unfortunate, not to say regrettable," announced Saladin calmly, "should such an occurrence happen again."

He motioned toward his turbaned servants, and immediately one of them came forth to refill their guest's cup with wine.

Tripoli smiled an acknowledgment, took a long leisurely sip and studied the chessboard between them. He knew, of course, that he himself was being closely studied as well.

"The debacle all those months ago at Ascalon was a mistake and will not be repeated, I assure you." The Count easily moved his Queen into the position he wanted and smiled again. "Checkmate," he said with satisfaction.

Saladin, as always, accepted his defeat graciously. Indeed, he had planned it. Let the Christian Count think himself clever! There were other games to play and higher stakes to win. He leaned back against his cushions and took a drink from his own goblet. It was not wine, however. The Muslim religion forbade such "base immorality."

He came straight to the point. "Eliminate the boy," he said, "let me take Jerusalem, and you shall become one of the wealthiest men in Syria."

Tripoli said nothing. He had no intention of being cornered. Perhaps he could yet get the Throne for himself by other means. Force of arms maybe. He didn't necessarily have to give the Kingdom to Saladin.

"The boy is sickly and will not live forever," he replied at last. "I daresay his heiress, the future Queen, will prove a much easier piece to move in our little game." It all depended so much on whom Sibyl would marry, weak king or strong. But Tripoli was a patient man.

"I want Jerusalem now," said the Sultan.

The Count merely brushed the statement aside with a sweep of his hand. "Jerusalem, my friend, shall always be there for the taking."

✎ Chapter Twenty-Three ✎

"THIS isn't working, Agnes. I tell you, if the King hasn't agreed by now, he never will!"

Lady Agnes de Courtenay merely smiled at the middle-aged nobleman beside her and set her squirming grandson down on the patch of soft grass. "Don't fret so much, Aimery dear. Everything will work out fine. Just trust me." She handed the little Prince his toy wooden horse, then settled back on the garden bench.

Sir Aimery de Lusignan heaved a sigh. "How can you just sit there when all our plans are being scattered to the four winds right before our eyes?"

"I really think you're overreacting, darling. If you ask me, things are falling into place beautifully." The Countess's gaze traveled to the beach below the terrace, where Sibyl and Guy were walking hand in hand. "Just look at them," she said. "Cooing like a pair of doves! Your young brother obviously adores her."

"It's not Guy I'm worried about, for heaven's sake! It's Baldwin! Unless he eventually consents, they can't get married. That's all there is to it."

Lady Agnes reached toward the platter on the nearby table and took a portion of cake. Absently she began to nibble on it. "Leave Baldwin to me," she said. "I can handle my own son."

"Just like you were able to handle his father?"

The Countess ignored the jibe. "Baldwin is a mere boy,

not yet nineteen. Amalric was a different story altogether. And I can't understand why you French-born
Frenchmen get so worked up over the most trifling of set-
backs."

"I'll tell you why, Agnes," Aimery replied. "It's because
the King is adamantly opposed to Guy courting his sister.
Is that what you would call a trifling setback?"

Agnes shrugged, undaunted. It was true, yes, Baldwin
had shown himself more discerning than she would have
liked to give him credit for, and he had obviously seen
Guy de Lusignan for what he really was. But she wasn't
one to be put off easily.

Besides, up to this point everything had gone so
smoothly. Not only had Aimery been able to persuade his
shallow younger brother to leave behind his estates in
France and come to Outremer, but his arrival had been
so cleverly planned that neither he nor Sibyl had any
idea that Agnes was the one behind it all. Indeed, Sibyl
was so full of herself that the silly girl actually believed
it was she who had launched the whole scheme of using
Sir Guy as the next King of Jerusalem.

Oh, yes, Guy was exactly the kind of puppet they were
after! Put a dandy like him on the Throne and there was
no limit to the power Agnes might achieve. Her daughter,
so it seemed, was thinking along the same lines, but little
did Sibyl realize that she too was but a pawn in the game.

The only problem, of course, remained Baldwin.

As if reading the Countess's thoughts, Aimery spoke
up. "And how exactly, may I ask, do you propose to dupe
the King?"

Agnes smiled. "Oh, I don't think for a moment he can
be duped. But there are other ways, you know, to deal
with the pious Baldwin. . . ."

❧ Chapter Twenty-Four ❧

IT was by force of habit that Theo took his place among the novices as the monks filed quietly into the Chapter Room. He clasped his hands beneath his white mantle and lowered his eyes to the floor.

Next to him, someone gave him a nudge. "Other side, Brother Theo."

Of course. He belonged with the professed Religious now. He'd taken his final vows. He crossed to the row of Templars opposite and noticed with mild curiosity that four new faces were amongst them. Well, he shouldn't be too surprised. It probably just meant that some of his own brothers were being sent to a different garrison.

After a few moments, the Superior of the Gaza Monastery entered the room and immediately the men all knelt down. Theo knew the routine by heart now. Prayers, a spiritual exhortation, the chapter of faults. Then came any news of the war, instructions, patrol assignments, that sort of thing. Life had been uneventful lately; it seemed as if Saladin had not yet recovered from his great losses at Ascalon, and fighting had ceased in most parts of the Kingdom.

But it wasn't news of the Sultan that Theo anxiously awaited. No, it was news of Dwin. Earlier in the week the knights had been asked to pray for him; their King had been suddenly seized by mysterious and violent stomach pains, for which the doctors could find neither cause nor remedy. He was expected to die any day now.

Theo's own best friend, actually dying. And he couldn't even be there to say good-bye. It had been nearly a year now since they had fought side by side on that blood-drenched desert plain. God had let them be part of a miracle, had spared both their lives and allowed them to be together one last time. But now Theo knew they would never see each other again.

He closed his eyes and tried not to think about it, tried to force away the image of poor Dwin on his deathbed, so helpless and ravaged by disease and pain. The way his friend's face had looked when he'd last seen him was branded into his memory, and Theo felt his heart contract with sorrow.

Leprosy. What a horrible and humiliating way to have to go! Yet, deep inside, Theo realized it was perhaps a fitting end for a King who had always striven to imitate the Crucified Divine Sovereign. Dwin was so good, so pure, and great would be his reward in Heaven. Theo would count himself most blessed if only his own death, someday, could be as holy and resigned as Baldwin's would no doubt be.

But today the Prior seemed to have no new word of their Monarch's condition. No, he was merely droning off a list of brothers' names which no doubt had nothing to do with Theo. He stopped listening and started instead to pray for Baldwin.

After a few moments he became aware of an awkward silence. He glanced up and realized everyone was looking at him.

"Brother Theodore," the Superior repeated patiently. His name must have been called!

He quickly stepped up next to the other three knights who had been summoned to the front: Brother Geoffrey,

Brother Marcel and Brother Bernard.

"You four are being replaced here at Gaza. I apologize for such short notice, but you've been chosen for an immediate posting at another of our garrisons."

Theo tried not to show any reaction. He had become so used to Gaza that he never even thought about being transferred elsewhere. Beside him, Brother Geoffrey also stood silent and motionless, but Theo knew that adjusting to a new home wouldn't be easy for him either. He had been here for over a decade.

"Assemble your personal things," the Prior continued, "and be ready to ride out within half an hour."

✑ Chapter Twenty-Five ✑

BROTHER Geoffrey was sweltering under the steel of his hauberk. Several times during the last couple of days he had been tempted to dispense the four of them from wearing their coats of mail, but he'd always stopped himself before granting permission. He knew the rules. Ride fully armored and in silence, no matter how scorching the desert heat nor how long the journey. But the other three didn't complain, and they had managed to make good time. It could have been a lot worse.

Their destination, it turned out, was Jerusalem. They arrived in daylight, thus the gates of the city were open. As Templars they passed through without question. But Geoffrey didn't need to look up to know that the turrets were teeming with guards. Other Templars, no doubt. With the Monarch dying, or possibly even dead by now, the Kingdom was in a state of uncertainty. And uncertainty always translated into potential danger.

Compared to Gaza, the capital city was an entirely different world. The noises, the sights, even the aromas were overwhelming as they rode through the crowded streets, and Geoffrey could see how easy it would be for worldlings to lose their souls amidst all the distractions and pleasures. But the four monks kept their eyes guarded and headed straight for the Temple.

Geoffrey noticed that beside him Brother Theo had

quickened his horse's stride, and he had to nudge his own mount into a swift trot in order to keep up. As a matter of fact, his youngest brother had been acting this way during the entire journey, and more than once Geoffrey had ordered him to slow down before they ended up needlessly destroying four good stallions. Why Theo was so eager to reach their new home, Geoffrey couldn't imagine.

When at last they entered the monastery stable yard, a group of sergeants, the unknighted servile branch of the Templars, were already waiting to take their mounts. The four riders had obviously been spotted long before they had reached the walls of Jerusalem. Geoffrey wiped the sweat from his eyes, dismounted with his three brothers and looked around for someone in charge. There was no point asking the sergeants about anything; they were never told the more important business of the knights. He was grateful when he saw an officer walking across the yard toward them.

"Greetings in Christ," the Templar welcomed when he reached them.

"Greetings in Christ, Brother," Geoffrey answered for them all.

"His lordship, Master Odo, is awaiting your arrival. He wishes you to report to him immediately for your instructions."

Geoffrey felt his heart sink. It would have been so nice to have a few decent hours of sleep first before facing someone of such importance as the Grand Master of the Order. But it wasn't his place to argue. "Where do we go?" he asked.

The Jerusalem Templar looked apologetic. He could see how hot and weary they were. "Your orders are to report directly to the Royal Palace."

"The Royal Palace?" Geoffrey repeated, bewildered. "Surely there must be some mistake."

"There's no mistake, I assure you. You're meant to go to His Majesty's private chambers. Master Odo will meet you there."

Geoffrey just stared in disbelief.

Brother Theo practically leapt forward, then caught himself in time and stood still. Geoffrey was their leader and Theo knew he must wait for him. But he seemed like he was about to burst.

Geoffrey, however, wasn't quite as willing to go. He glanced at their once white surcoats, now filthy after three days and nights in the desert. "You must be joking!" he said flatly. "We can't appear before His Majesty looking like a band of outlaws!" He had already done it once, of course, when he, Bernard and Marcel had warned the King of Saladin's invasion from Egypt, but that had been entirely different! "At least give us ten minutes to get cleaned up and changed," he insisted. "I refuse to offer such an insult to my Sovereign."

The Jerusalem officer raised his hands helplessly. "I'm sorry, Brother. Orders are orders."

"I don't believe this!"

Next to him, Brother Theo could contain himself no longer. "Come on, let's go. He won't mind, I'm sure of it!"

Geoffrey turned and shot Theo a reproachful look, but the younger knight didn't seem to notice. "Please, Brother Geoffrey," he pleaded. "He's dying!"

Well, Geoffrey thought with annoyance, on Master Odo's head be it if the King threw them straight out! He turned his gaze toward the Palace across the Temple court, then looked back at the officer. "Surely, Brother, you can't expect us to find our own way into the King's private rooms! This is crazy. Get us an escort."

But to Geoffrey's astonishment, Brother Theo grabbed him by the arm and started to head off. "Just follow me," he said. "I know exactly where to go."

∽ Chapter Twenty-Six ∾

I T seemed to Theo like forever ago that he had lived within this palace as a page, but he still knew the maze of corridors by heart. Every so often he and his brothers ran into a chamberlain, and a few naturally tried to stop them, but at Geoffrey's curt, "King's business," the four dirty and unescorted knights were allowed to pass unhindered.

Beside him, Geoffrey now moved closer. "It's taken me awhile, I admit," he said quietly, "but I've finally caught on. The way you've been acting all this time must mean you're a personal friend of His Majesty. Why didn't you simply tell me?"

Theo hesitated. "I didn't think I was supposed to. I mean, a monk is meant to be above human attachments, let alone boasting of them."

His older brother glanced at him and nodded with approval. "Maybe you know, then," he said, "why we've been called here. Because I certainly don't."

Theo shook his head. "I have no idea." If it had been himself alone, then it would be understandable. That would obviously mean Master Odo was allowing him to see Dwin one last time. But why the other three? And why wouldn't they be returning to Gaza?

Whatever the case, Theo knew he was either about to watch his best friend die or else see him lying dead in a coffin, and he was immensely grateful that someone of

Brother Geoffrey's strength was here with him.

They reached the King's quarters; a chamberlain was expecting them at the door. He led them inside, but before he ushered them into the bedchamber, Geoffrey put a hand on Theo's arm and held him back.

"It's been a whole year since you've seen him," he warned. "Leprosy can progress very quickly. You do realize that?"

Theo nodded, but he knew he had better brace himself before entering that room. At least at Ascalon he'd had his own face hidden behind a solid steel helm and Dwin had been unable to see his reaction. But now he was going to have to do this unmasked, and he begged God that no horror would show.

He stepped back so his older brothers could enter first, in order of rank, then determinedly locked his gaze on the floor and followed them in. The room, surprisingly, was empty of attendants. Even the chamberlain departed and closed the door. There were two other Templars in the room, as their Holy Rule forbade them to go anywhere alone. One, Theo knew, would be Master Odo, the other an officer.

From the corner of his eye he saw the bed and realized with relief that Baldwin was at least still alive. Yet he didn't trust himself to look just yet. Silently he slipped into line beside Brother Geoffrey. He didn't belong there, of course. Being the youngest, he should have taken his position at the far end, next to Marcel. But he hoped Master Odo would indulge him, just this once.

In unison all four knights bowed, straightened, and placed their hands upon the hilts of their swords. In that stance, they dutifully transformed themselves into statues.

Sir Odo spoke, and Theo was startled to hear a trace of

amusement in his voice. "You must forgive them, Sire," he said. "They don't normally go about looking like highwaymen, I assure you."

Theo heard the King let out a little laugh. It was very weak, yes, but still the same laugh he'd always known. Maybe Dwin wasn't going to die after all. Surely no one could be amused when in the throes of a death agony!

The Master continued. "Allow me, Sire, if you will, to refresh your memory. I realize it's been quite some time since you were first introduced to these men. Brother Geoffrey Chateauneuf . . ."

Geoffrey inclined his head respectfully. "Sire." Then to Sir Odo, "My lord."

"Brother Geoffrey is the senior knight here. He's been with the Gaza Chapter for eleven years, and I believe him best suited for the command of this post." Sir Odo paused, then went on. "Brother Bernard Labouisse. Six years in the Order. He's served at several of our garrisons and fought with us at Damascus."

"Sire. My lord."

"Brother Marcel Jourdanne. He entered at Gaza nearly five years ago."

Again, the same filial reply.

Theo knew he was going to have to raise his eyes soon. Dwin could see him standing here, plain as day, and to refuse to look at him would not only be lacking in respect but also terribly hurtful.

He heard Sir Odo continue. "And, of course, our youngest knight, Brother Theodore de Thierceville." He chuckled and added, "I don't believe any introduction is necessary in his case."

Theo inclined his head. "Sire." Then he looked at the bed, and the two friends smiled at each other. It happened so naturally that Theo didn't even have to think about it.

But he instantly went cold inside. *Dwin's entire face!* It had looked ghastly enough a year ago, but now it was disfigured beyond recognition. Theo felt sick with shock and anguish. He quickly dropped his gaze to the floor.

Just stay a statue! he ordered himself. *Show no reaction! That's what Templars are trained to do.*

He felt Brother Geoffrey give him a nudge and realized that he had forgotten to acknowledge his Superior. "My lord!" he blurted out.

There was a brief silence, and inwardly Theo cringed. Well, he had certainly made a mess of that! Had poor Dwin actually seen his shocked expression? Theo was sure he must have.

To his relief, Sir Odo continued, this time addressing the knights. "You're no doubt wondering why you've been summoned here so suddenly from Gaza. I've chosen you for this special assignment because each one of you has shown outstanding loyalty and self-sacrifice toward His Majesty the King and the cause of this Realm. Were it not for you four, I daresay Saladin would be in possession of this palace."

Theo tried to pay attention to the Master's words, but all he could think about was how terribly deformed Dwin was. Was it truly his friend lying there? He who had always been the perfect prince, so majestic in bearing, so striking in appearance, was now hardly more than a living corpse!

"As you all know," Sir Odo was saying, "His Majesty's life has been greatly feared for these last several days. Yet we can thank God for sparing him, as it seems the danger has finally passed. I'm afraid, however, that our beloved King is not entirely safe." He paused, then lowered his voice slightly. "Just between those of us here in this room, there is some suspicion that His Majesty was intentionally poisoned."

Well, that certainly jerked Theo's attention back! All four knights gave a start.

"Poison!" Brother Marcel exclaimed. "But who would—" He stopped himself and shut his mouth.

"We have absolutely no proof," Baldwin said quietly, speaking for the first time and with obvious effort. "It may not be true at all. The doctors don't know for sure."

So like him, Theo thought, to try to preserve the good names of others, even when he was so sick he could hardly talk!

"Perhaps," Sir Odo agreed. "But my mind would be more at ease were I to know that His Majesty was surrounded from now on by a team of trustworthy bodyguards. I've been able to persuade him of this, and I could think of no braver or more devoted knights for the job than the four of you."

Theo looked in surprise at his Grand Master. It had been Sir Odo himself who had sent him away from Jerusalem for the express purpose of separating him from Dwin. But the older man merely smiled and said, "Your orders, my sons, are very simple: Protect the King. Within the bounds of Christian morals, I care not by what means nor at what cost. Just do it."

The four Templars bowed their heads in acceptance.

"Of course, of necessity, you will live here in the Palace, but I expect you to continue your community life and the observance of our Holy Rule within these confines. The room adjoining this has been arranged as your sleeping quarters, and a chapel and dining area have also been set up for your private use. You will come to the Temple in pairs for attendance at Mass, Chapter, and your daily practice in arms. As for everything else, Brother Geoffrey will use his discretion and may consider that my authority as Religious Superior becomes his own if, in his judgment, circumstances so dictate. Yet I urge that at least two of you remain with the King at all times. Is that understood?"

"Yes, my lord," they answered as one.

"Very well, then." Sir Odo gave Brother Geoffrey a look.

The knight knew what was expected of him. He strode forward to the bed and bent on one knee. Then, taking the King's gloved hand in his own, he kissed it and said, "I am thy true subject, Sire. I swear my service and fealty to thee."

He rose and stepped back into line. In order of age, the next two Templars did the same.

It was Theo's turn. He went to the bed and knelt, but before he could speak the oath of homage, Baldwin reached out and took both his hands. "I'm glad you're here, Theo," he whispered. His grasp was unbelievably feeble, his breathing labored.

"I'm glad to be here too, Dwin," Theo answered softly. "You have no idea how hard I've been praying for you." He squeezed the leper's hands as tightly as he could, begging God that Dwin might feel something of the pressure despite his numbness. Then he kissed one of those gloves and promised, "I am thy true subject, Sire. I swear my service and fealty to thee."

Theo felt hot tears begin to sting his eyes, but fought them back so that Baldwin wouldn't notice. He would get used to that horribly decayed face in time; he knew he would. And, together with his three brothers, he would make certain no enemy would ever touch their beloved Sovereign again.

✍ Chapter Twenty-Seven ✍

"**I** CAN'T do it," Baldwin said with mounting dread. "There is no way I can face all those people in there looking the way I do."

"You look fine, Sire," came the voice beside him, now so familiar after three months of constant companionship. "You should stop worrying about it all the time."

The King let out a weary sigh. "Don't lie to me, Brother Marcel, please," he begged. "I've had to listen to deception since the day I was crowned and I don't need to hear it from my friends as well."

At his other side, Theo gently intervened. "There's hardly anyone in there, Sire. Just a few pages, your Uncle Jocelin, that Aimery fellow your mother's always dragging around with her these days, and a couple of his squires. That's about it."

Baldwin knew Theo had already guessed: his vision was starting to fail. He tried so hard not to let them know, but it was impossible for him to hide anything from Theo or Geoffrey.

"Mother's in there," Baldwin said.

"It'll be all right," Theo reassured.

Baldwin hated this, but he had little choice. He and his attendants had traveled all this way to Jaffa to meet his mother, at her insistence; he could hardly tell his entire retinue that he had changed his mind and they were heading straight back to Jerusalem.

107

He drew in a deep breath and put on that air of authority and self-assurance which he'd trained himself to assume so well for years now. He stepped into the hall, surrounded by his four faithful guards. Behind them trailed two of his pages, but the rest of his escort had been dismissed. His mother apparently wished to see him in private.

At his entrance, the Countess and her small gathering of companions fell quiet and rose to their feet. Baldwin made his way to the chair set up on a low platform and sat down. The pages withdrew to the side, but the Templars stepped to the four corners of the throne and took up their usual silent stance.

"My darling Baldwin!" Lady Agnes trilled with obvious insincerity. "What a relief to see you looking so well! We've all been worried sick for months!" She made no move, however, to embrace her son, but kept a safe distance between them. "I trust your journey was not too tiring?"

It had been. Extremely. Baldwin's strength had not completely returned; he doubted that it ever would. He felt so drained, and it took an effort to focus his eyes on his mother standing before him. She kept fading into darkness, then returning again. "My attendants outdid themselves on the journey, Mother," he answered. "Please do begin."

The Countess arranged a smile on her face and froze it there. "I desire to speak to you in private, Baldwin. I thought I had made that clear."

Baldwin knew, of course, that his mother was referring to the Templars. Yet, he fixed his gaze instead on the other men in the room and said innocently, "I grant you leave."

There was an awkward silence. Jocelin de Courtenay

and Aimery de Lusignan glanced at each other and shifted uncomfortably. They obviously had no intention of leaving.

"You may go," the King repeated.

His uncle cleared his throat. "Sire, we wish to speak with you as well."

So, they were going to gang up on him. He'd suspected as much.

"As you wish," he said. "Speak."

No one said a word. Aimery's few squires shuffled a bit further into the background, as if they wanted no part of this. The pages, likewise, seemed to be looking for an escape.

"Yes?" Baldwin prompted.

His mother, however, was not going to be bullied. This was her residence, after all. She glared at the knights surrounding her son and gave the command herself. "Leave. Now. All of you."

No reaction.

Agnes de Courtenay noticed exactly the position of their hands. Folded together and resting ever so casually on the hilts of their swords. It made her feel uneasy.

"I said, leave."

Still no movement.

She turned sharply to the King. "What kind of insolent subjects are these?!" she demanded. "They refuse to obey the simplest of orders!"

"Oh, I wouldn't say that," Baldwin answered mildly. "I find they obey quite well." He glanced at the table beside him, but was unable to discern whether or not his mother had provided the customary goblet of wine. Then he noticed a sudden and embarrassed scramble amongst the pages and realized that, indeed, she had overlooked, or else purposely neglected, this most basic courtesy. He wasn't sure which.

Within a matter of seconds, one of her pages appeared with the missing drink. Before Baldwin could reach for it, however, Brother Bernard calmly intercepted the cup. Baldwin saw the Templar take a cautious sip, much to his mother's horror.

"Why, the audacity!" he heard her shriek. "How dare this knight imply that I would actually poison my own child!"

Brother Bernard was unperturbed. He waited for a few seconds, then, satisfied, passed the goblet to Baldwin and became a statue once again.

It was Geoffrey who spoke. "We have our orders, my lady."

She pierced them both with a vicious look, but before she could give further vent to her indignation, Baldwin decided to step in. "I'm sure you asked me to come here for a reason, Mother. No doubt it's something important. Would you like to tell me what it is?"

"I'll tell you just as soon as you clear out these four brutes, and not a moment before!"

Aimery de Lusignan spoke for the first time. "We refuse, Sire, to tolerate them eavesdropping on the affairs of this court."

"Dismiss them at once, Baldwin. I mean it!"

The young King had to smile. "I'm afraid you'll find, Mother, that they're not so easy to get rid of." He took a sip of the wine, and was instantly grateful for its coolness. He felt tired and weak and wanted to get this audience over with. "Please," he insisted, "what would you like to discuss?"

His mother only glared at him. She was going to be stubborn.

Jocelin de Courtenay, however, was growing impatient. He took over from his sister and began. "Sire, we are your most loyal subjects and desire only what is best for this Realm. I speak for the few of us here in this room and also for my fellow barons."

Baldwin felt his muscles tense. An alarm was triggered somewhere within. It was easy to guess where this was leading.

"Yes, Uncle," he said. "Go on."

"You have fulfilled your duties toward the Kingdom admirably and have our deepest obeisance. We believe, however, that the issue of your health is one which cannot be ignored any longer." Sir Jocelin looked quickly at Aimery de Lusignan, as if seeking reassurance of the other's support, then dealt the blow. "Sire, we strongly urge you to yield the Throne."

The four Templars instantly stiffened. But they had no business interfering and they knew it.

Baldwin closed his eyes. The words were crushing. Yield his Throne and give it to another. For a long moment he could not answer. Were it up to him, there was nothing he would like more than to retire from the world and seek admission among the Lazar Knights of St. Ladre, the monastic Order to which leprous noblemen were sent. There he could at least spend what little time was left to him in prayer and peace. But Baldwin knew such was not the Divine Will. God Almighty, whose ways were beyond human comprehension, who chose the weak to confound the strong, had placed this Kingdom into the keeping of a leper, and keep it Baldwin would until God Himself ordained otherwise.

At last the young King opened his eyes and searched among the cloudy grayness for the figure of his uncle. It took a few seconds for him to focus. He was growing so very faint, sitting here in this stifling heat. If only he could get a breath of fresh air.

Next to him he sensed a slight movement and knew without looking that Theo had moved in closer. Theo, as always, could tell when his little strength was failing.

Baldwin, however, fought to ignore his disorientation. "I will abdicate," he answered softly, "only when my sister Sibyl is wed to an honorable and worthy prince, one whose sole concern in ruling this Kingdom will be the glory of God and the good of the Realm. To such a man and no other shall I surrender my Crown."

He saw his mother turn to Aimery de Lusignan and knew it was the cue for the other man to enter the game. Nervously the Frenchman stepped forward, a trickle of sweat forming on his brow. "Sire," he said with an effort, "regarding this issue of . . . uh . . . marriage. My brother Sir Guy most humbly begs thy Majesty for the hand of Her Highness the Princess Sibyl. I entreat—"

"Forgive me, my lord, but the answer is no."

"Sibyl and Guy love each other!" Lady Agnes blurted. "How can you be so cruel as to deny them their happiness together?"

It was a ludicrous argument, and everyone in the room must have known it. Those of royal birth were seldom allowed to wed for the fulfillment of love. A sad fact of life, Baldwin realized, but that's the way it had always been. Besides, it was obvious that Sibyl harbored no true affection for Guy. She saw the man purely as a puppet, a cowardly toy to use in furthering her own ambitions. Lady Agnes and Sir Aimery, likewise, desired the union for exactly the same reason. Guy de Lusignan had not the heart of a king and everyone could see it. Even his own elder brother!

"I'm sorry, Mother," Baldwin said. "I refuse to consent."

Jocelin de Courtenay tried next. "Sire, with all due respect, you would be most wise to reconsider this matter. The barons and myself—"

"It has been considered deeply, I assure you." They were fading into obscurity again. Baldwin fought to bring them back. "I've sent an urgent appeal to our Holy Father the Pope," he told them, hearing the strain in his own voice. "If this Kingdom is to withstand the assaults of the enemy, then we need help desperately from the west. If any prince in Europe is brave and noble enough to lead a third Crusade here to the Holy Land, then to that man have I already promised both my Crown and my sister's hand in marriage."

A shocked murmur rippled through the group of pages and squires, and they seemed to cower against the wall. The two noblemen paled slightly, and Lady Agnes squared her shoulders.

Baldwin realized they all knew something he didn't. A terrible silence fell upon the room.

Something was wrong. Terribly, dreadfully wrong.

"Mother," he asked, "what's going on?"

He heard her let out a snort of disgust. "You stupid and foolish boy!" she snarled. "You should never have promised that which is no longer yours to give! Our next king has already been chosen, and neither you nor the Pope can do a single thing about it."

Baldwin sat forward, his heart starting to race. "What are you saying?" he demanded.

His mother raised her chin in defiance. "Your sister is already wed. She has been the lawful wife of His Highness Prince Guy de Lusignan since last Easter, and he'll inherit your Kingdom, whether you like it or not!"

✐ Chapter Twenty-Eight ✐

(The Banks of the Jordan River, several months later)

"THEO," Baldwin asked, "are you still here?"
Theo had his hand securely on top of the King's own, helping him hold his reins, and their horses were so close they were touching. But he knew Dwin was becoming disoriented after hours of riding through this torturous desert heat with so little rest or water.

"Of course I'm here, Sire. I'm right beside you." He gave Baldwin's hand a hard squeeze, so that Dwin would be reassured. He'd learned by now that roughness was the only way to make the King feel.

"Where is Brother Geoffrey?"

The other knight answered for himself. "Riding on your left, Sire. Do you need to stop and rest?"

The sound of their voices so close seemed to calm him and Baldwin shook his head. "No, I'll be fine. Thank you."

The two Templars exchanged a look. He didn't appear fine to either of them. Geoffrey reached for his own canteen. There were only a few swallows of stale water left in it, but that would be better than nothing at all. Theo pulled the King's mount to a halt, and Brothers Marcel and Bernard reined in as well. Then Geoffrey placed the vessel in the feeble gloved hands of the Sovereign and gently closed his fingers around it.

"Drink, Sire."

114

Baldwin smiled weakly, but handed the canteen back. "No, Brother Geoffrey. My whole army has ridden as long as I have, and I will share in their hardships. Drink it yourself."

Geoffrey sighed. They'd been through all this before and he knew it was a losing battle.

Theo knew it too. No point even arguing. He simply urged the horses forward once again.

"Saladin's nephew," Baldwin said. "Can you still see him out there?"

Theo turned his head and studied the Muslim troops riding parallel to their own. "Unfortunately, Sire, he's clear as day." The two armies had been moving like this for miles, the River Jordan the only thing separating them.

"What do you make of their position now?" Baldwin asked. "Any change?"

Theo left it to his more experienced brother to answer. "There still appears to be no hostility in their movements," Geoffrey replied. "But that, of course, means little."

Baldwin agreed. He closed his eyes and tried to picture the scene. He trusted Theo to guide his mount, and he could think more clearly when he didn't have to struggle to discern his surroundings. If only he knew what the Infidel was up to!

He wished his squires would hurry up and return with advice from Sir Odo. He'd sent them to the flank of the army, where the main body of Templars was positioned closest to the point of potential danger. If there was anyone's opinion the King wanted right now, it was that of the wise Grand Master.

The knights, Baldwin knew, were all exhausted from the heat. Their water supplies were failing, yet he'd felt compelled to issue an order that no one approach the river, lest the movement be taken by the enemy as a sign of attack.

Saladin's nephew, Faruk-Shah, had been besieging the Templar fortress at Jacob's Ford, but had backed off when the Crusaders had rallied to the rescue. Now the Muslims seemed to be retreating, yet Baldwin had decided to follow in order to ensure their withdrawal was sincere. Now he wondered if he should instead call off his men. This didn't seem a good place for a battle.

But perhaps the Templar Master would counsel otherwise. Baldwin would wait and see.

"Sire," informed Brother Geoffrey, breaking into his thoughts, "Sir Gerard de Ridford is approaching. The Count of Tripoli and Guy de Lusignan are with him, and by the looks of it, neither of them is too happy."

No one was allowed to honor Guy with the title of "Prince." Baldwin adamantly refused to acknowledge his brother-in-law as his rightful successor.

Once again, Theo pulled in Baldwin's mount, and the rest of the vanguard straggled to a stop behind them. The three newcomers rode up, and Gerard de Ridford got straight to the point. "Sire," he began, "as you requested, Master Odo and I have been in counsel with our officers. We urge you to order an immediate attack, before the enemy crosses that rise. One good hit, in and out, and we could easily crush them."

Baldwin was surprised. This wasn't what he'd been expecting to hear. Before he could reply, however, the Count of Tripoli exploded, "Sire, you must not listen to such insane advice! Call off our men and let the enemy go in peace!"

De Ridford shot the Count a savage look. "Tripoli always wants the Infidel to escape, Sire. Haven't you noticed?"

Baldwin had, indeed, noticed. But he also knew De Ridford and Tripoli were still locked in their private feud, as they had been for years, and they refused to agree on the least issue.

De Ridford didn't bother to wait for Baldwin's reply, but instead continued: "In total, we have nearly four hundred Templars here in our command. Master Odo seeks your permission to send them all in. Allow us to attack in our full force, and I assure you, Sire, you'll not regret it. Faruk-Shah would be a prisoner of considerable value, and he's right there for the taking."

Baldwin turned to survey the enemy, but his eyes refused to cooperate. Their army was but a swarming dark cloud on the edge of his vision and he could make practically nothing of it.

"There are so few of us in comparison," he said, "and our men have been without sufficient water for hours." He wasn't sure he agreed with Sir Odo this time. His instincts warned him this might be a mistake. After all, even the most experienced of warriors could sometimes err in judgment.

De Ridford, however, persisted. "May I remind you, Sire, that at Ascalon you had but three hundred against thirty thousand. And yet a mere thirty Templars won for you that day."

Geoffrey glanced at the King, then turned to his Marshal. "If I may, my lord. Ascalon was an entirely different situation. The Sultan's troops were—"

"Thank you, Brother Geoffrey," De Ridford cut him off curtly. "I've heard all about it, believe me."

"No," Baldwin said. "Let him speak. He was there."

The Marshal couldn't hide his annoyance, but he nonetheless inclined his head in submission to the King. "Go ahead, Brother."

Geoffrey continued. "The enemy, unlike now, were completely disorganized. It was a surprise attack, and God gave the victory, not we few Templars."

De Ridford glared at him and opened his mouth to speak, but Guy de Lusignan barged in. "I stand with Tripoli. To attack would be suicide!"

"I did not ask for your opinion, Sir Guy," Baldwin said sharply. "You have my leave."

Sibyl's husband stiffened, but ignored the King's dismissal. "I was merely trying to point out," he continued tersely, "that if we order an—"

Theo couldn't restrain himself. "If *His Majesty* orders, you mean!"

"We're wasting valuable time!" De Ridford barked. "Sire, let us go in. Now! Master Odo and I have already positioned our knights into battle formation. They but await my signal for the charge."

For once, Baldwin was at a loss. If only he could see the situation for himself! He gazed out in the direction of the opposing army, but it was of no use. His diseased eyes failed him.

"Theo," he began helplessly, "what is your—"

"Brother Theodore has absolutely no training in military science," the Templar Marshal snapped. "To consult the opinion of a young and inexperienced knight is most uncharacteristic of you, Sire."

Baldwin knew it was true. He trusted Theo with his life, but in this matter, his faithful friend was of no help. "Sir Odo, you're sure, urges this attack?" he asked De Ridford.

"Absolutely. It's the chance of a lifetime to capture one of Saladin's own kin. With him in our possession, our bargaining power would be tremendous."

Baldwin felt dizzy; his mind was becoming unclear. He

strongly suspected that this was neither the time nor the place for a battle, but he didn't know if he should trust his own feelings.

He searched the blurry faces around him for guidance, but the decision rested with him alone.

Four hundred Templars . . .

Sir Odo's prompting . . .

Saladin's nephew in his hands!

"All right," he reluctantly agreed. He fixed his eyes on the figure of De Ridford. "Send your men in." Then, to Tripoli, "My lord, assemble the secular knights into position and tell them to await my orders."

For a moment it seemed as if Tripoli would refuse to obey, but then both he and Guy angrily jerked on their reins and rode off to do the King's bidding.

De Ridford smiled. "We will not disappoint you, Sire. A priceless treasure will be ours before this day is through." Then he turned to Baldwin's bodyguards. "Arm yourselves for the charge and join your brothers."

"I'm sorry, my lord," Geoffrey said, "but we cannot leave His Majesty."

The Marshal ignored him and motioned instead to the squires waiting behind. They came forward, already prepared with lances and helmets and shields for the four knights.

Geoffrey tried again. "Our personal orders, I believe, are to remain with the King."

De Ridford bristled. "Not this time, Brother Geoffrey. I certainly heard no exceptions from Master Odo. Take up your arms this instant, or I shall be forced to deal with you according to the breach of your holy vows of obedience."

Startled, both Brothers Bernard and Marcel accepted their lances and strapped on their shields. Theo, however, kept his eyes on Geoffrey, awaiting his lead.

"My lord," Geoffrey persisted, "I fear there may be some mistake. Perhaps not, but I request your leave to speak with Master Odo. It will take less than ten minutes."

"There is no mistake," the Marshal growled, "and we haven't ten minutes to spare! Time is of the essence. I was distinctly instructed to prepare our men for an immediate full frontal charge. That means everyone."

Geoffrey cast a look in the distance toward the rest of the Templars gathered on the edge of the army. Maybe De Ridford was right, and the Master, in this particular circumstance, desired them to fight rather than guard the King. Deep inside, Geoffrey feared an attack was unwise, but if such was Sir Odo's command, then they must certainly acquiesce. He realized that the Marshal was correct in one thing at least: if they were going to charge, there was no time to waste. The enemy's vanguard was already disappearing between two hills and would soon be out of sight.

Theo broke the silence, appealing directly to the King. "Sire, surely you can insist that we—"

But Baldwin cut him off. "I have no authority to interfere with this, Theo. You know that. The Templar Order is autonomous by decree of the Pope and it's not within my power to override your superior's decisions. I'm sorry." He understood their problem, however, and gently added, "If it makes it any easier for you, I'm sure I'll be safe back here with the others. I would urge you to go."

Brother Geoffrey addressed the other three: "I can't imagine Master Odo forgetting our position. I can only assume that he wants us to fight. Looking at the situation, every Templar out there is going to make a difference. We'll go."

Theo nodded. Together he and Geoffrey accepted their

heavy lances and pulled on their helms. Satisfied, De Ridford turned and rode away.

Geoffrey spoke, his voice muffled beneath the steel. "God protect you, Sire."

"And you, my loyal friends."

"We'll be back, Dwin," Theo added softly. "You know we will."

Baldwin nodded, and silently prayed that he had made the right decision in permitting this bold attack.

But as he watched the blurry figures of his Templars spur their horses and gallop away, he wasn't at all sure he had.

⤫ Chapter Twenty-Nine ⤬

IT had been a trap. They'd been ambushed from the sides where Saladin's nephew had hidden his main force behind two hills, and Theo realized with a cold knot of fear that there were no Christian reinforcements on the way. The Templars were out here alone, and they had been trying to fight off this vast army by themselves for far too long already. Where were the rest of the Crusaders?!

The ground all around him was fast becoming slippery, and Theo knew it was with the blood of his brothers. They were being butchered, slaughtered in countless numbers, and absolutely no one was coming to help them!

His horse stumbled and he could feel himself lurching forward. The beast caught itself before falling, and Theo somehow managed to stay in the saddle. But he noticed that the leather strap of his shield had been broken. He couldn't hang onto it, and it dropped to the ground. Something was swinging straight at his head. Instinctively he raised an arm to block the gleaming blade and felt a bolt of agony as the ax sliced clean through the sleeve of his hauberk and ripped open his arm.

Next to him another horse collided with his own, nearly knocking him off, and he struggled to keep his balance. Then he realized it was Geoffrey, trying to cover him from the pelting rain of steel. He gratefully crouched beneath his brother's shield and fumbled to get a firmer grip on the slick hilt of his sword.

On his other side he heard an anguished scream; there was a spray of red onto his surcoat, and another Templar suddenly tumbled straight into his lap. There was a grotesque tangle of reins and limbs and crimson steel.

This was a bloodbath!

Please, dear God, he prayed, *please make someone get down here and help us!*

* * * * *

"What's happening?" Baldwin demanded. "What's going on down there?"

The Count of Tripoli stroked his beard thoughtfully and tried to decide what to say. "Well, Sire," he began, "it appears to me that the holy monks have committed a sin of rash judgment. They are in a somewhat regrettable situation."

Baldwin heard the voice of his uncle, Jocelin de Courtenay. "What Tripoli is really trying to say, Sire, is that the Templars are being absolutely massacred. Saladin's nephew was smarter than we gave him credit for. He had his main strength hidden behind those hills on either flank. None of us could even see them. They must have been waiting there all day."

"O sweet Jesus, have mercy," Baldwin whispered. "I've sent them straight to their deaths!"

"You've sent them nowhere," said Tripoli. "They chose to go."

"He's right, Sire. They have only themselves to blame. We all knew that one of these days their fierce pride would get them into a mess like this."

Baldwin felt a sickening pain in the pit of his stomach. "We've got to help them!" he said. "Get the first wave of reinforcements out there. *Now!*"

Neither of the barons moved.

"Sire," said his uncle, "I understand how you feel. There are a lot of good men among them, and it's not pleasant to sit here and watch them being so brutally slain. But with all due respect, to sacrifice the lives of others for the sake of the foolhardy Templars isn't quite what I would recommend."

"Sir Odo sent them to fight only for my Kingdom and God's glory. I'll be the one to decide what to do!" Baldwin closed his eyes and tried to calm the violent pounding of his heart. It was true—Master Odo had made a tragic mistake. If only Baldwin had listened to his own instincts! But it was too late now.

Yet he knew that God would help them. The Divine assistance would never fail, not if they put their complete trust in God's care.

He opened his eyes and turned to Tripoli. He had no choice but to rely on the man. "My cousin," he said, "I beg of you, for the love you bear Our Lord Jesus Christ, take my reins and help me lead this charge. My troops will follow if they know I am with them."

Both men stared at him.

"Sire," Jocelin de Courtenay protested, "you're in no condition whatsoever to—"

"If I must die, Uncle, then I will give my life for the cause of this holy war." He drew in a deep breath, fighting to clear his mind, trying to force his limbs to obey by sheer will power. "Please, Uncle," he insisted, "go and send out the order for my brave Crusaders to follow. Tell them God wills it, and He is on our side!"

*   *   *   *   *

Geoffrey knew they had to get out of here, and fast!

He hefted his sword back over his shoulder and thrust downward with all his might. The impact jarred his muscles, but he hit his mark and another Muslim went down under the massive hooves of his warhorse.

Geoffrey's eyes were stinging with sweat, and he looked around in desperation for Master Odo or Sir Gerard. Where on earth were they?! Someone had to order a retreat, now, before every last one of them was cut to pieces.

He knew that next to him Brother Theo was severely wounded. Amazingly, the younger knight continued to fight with what little strength he had left. Yet how much longer he could keep going, Geoffrey feared, was an entirely different matter.

Just hold on, he silently begged. *Don't die on me, little brother! Please!*

He steered his mount closer, as he'd done so many times already, and swung his sword at Theo's attacker. He fiercely fought the Saracen off, but noticed that his brother was no longer even trying to raise his own weapon. It was all he could do just to stay in the saddle. *He wasn't going to make it!*

In one swift move, Geoffrey reached over and grabbed Theo's reins, looping them over his own arm. Well, whatever happened, he'd make sure they stayed together! Then, out of the corner of his eye, he saw the signal he'd been waiting for. Some officer finally had enough brains in his head to realize they had to get away before it was too late. But as far as Geoffrey was concerned, it was already too late.

*   *   *   *   *

The Count of Tripoli had seen a lot of things in his day, but never anything quite like this. The remnant of the Templar army was wheeling around and flying back toward them with a frenzy that made the blood run cold in his veins.

But, an even more awesome sight, thousands of Saracens were galloping hard at their heels, heading straight for the main body of the Crusaders.

He opened his mouth to tell the King, but it wasn't necessary. Baldwin could hear for himself the terrifying high-pitched Muslim war cry and knew exactly what it meant.

"Get this army out of their way!" he yelled. "Order a retreat! *Now!*"

For the first time in his life, Count Raymond of Tripoli didn't need to be told twice. He dropped Baldwin's reins, whirled his own horse around in a panic and fled, leaving his King entirely defenseless and alone.

❦ Chapter Thirty ❧

THERE were so many dead to pray for. So many losses to mourn. The light from the moon shone on Geoffrey's sword where he had stabbed it into the earth, the shadow of its hilt a dark cross splayed upon the desert sand. The Templar knelt before it and silently begged God for mercy.

The stillness of the night was rent by a distant haunting cry. Geoffrey knew it was the moans of the dying, left in their agonies somewhere on the bloody plain. He bowed his head, the words of his prayers blurring in his mind. So many of his brothers were dead. His beloved King was dead. Hundreds of souls had gone to their Judgment and were perhaps now burning in the tormenting flames of Purgatory. Or even Hell.

A wave of anguish rose up within him, and with an effort he fought it down. The King's soul, at least, would be safe. Geoffrey could not doubt it. Baldwin had died pure, the death of the just.

But the loss still felt unbearable.

A vulture circled overhead, its screech piercing the night. Then it suddenly swooped down, and Geoffrey saw the shadow of its outspread wings make a momentary crescent over the cross.

So it would always be, he thought sadly. Would this war never end?

The bird lingered, then mercifully was gone.

Geoffrey knew he should go check on his brothers, but he was loathe to rise. He didn't want to leave the safe refuge of prayer. It would be so much easier to stay here on his knees, alone with God, alone with his own sorrow. But it wasn't that simple. If only it were.

Reluctantly he reached out and clasped the sword. Its hilt was sticky, the smell of blood still strong upon it. He pulled it from the earth and rose to his feet. Then he quietly made his way to where Brothers Marcel and Bernard were sprawled in the sand, their saddle blankets bundled beneath their heads. Their surcoats were ripped, their mail as bloodied as his own. In the darkness he was unable to see their faces clearly, but he realized with relief that they had at last fallen into an exhausted sleep.

How he'd even managed to find those two after that panicked retreat was practically a miracle in itself. Where all the other survivors had ended up was anyone's guess. Some, no doubt, had rejoined the main body of the army and were already on their way back to Jerusalem. Others had probably taken flight to the fortress at Jacob's Ford. A few, like themselves, were wandering out here in little bands near the River Jordan, unwilling to give up their search for missing friends.

Master Odo de Saint-Amand, he knew, had been captured by the enemy, leaving what was left of his flock with no true shepherd. As for Gerard de Ridford, who was presumably in command, he could be anywhere, dead or alive. And frankly, Geoffrey found it hard to care.

He left the sleeping pair and went to the campfire. It was hardly more than a few glowing embers now, but it had served its purpose and there was no point stoking it again. With his dagger he skewered a chunk of meat and removed it from the spit. Roasted horse flesh wasn't exactly his idea of a delicacy, but it would help keep them alive and that was what mattered.

He crossed over to his youngest brother, sitting nearby, and held out the knife. "You have to eat," he said. "Starving yourself won't bring the King back."

Theo only shook his head. Geoffrey could see that he was shivering, despite the heavy blanket wrapped around him. He'd lost a lot of blood. Too much. It had taken Geoffrey an eternity to finally stem the flow and sew everything back together, and even now he feared the wounds might reopen at any time. If only Theo would just lie down and keep still.

Instead, he started to rise. "I haven't said my Office yet."

Geoffrey gently pushed him back down. "You're dispensed. You have to rest." Exhausted, Theo sank again to the ground.

Theo spoke again. "He'd still be alive if only we hadn't left him. Sir Gerard—"

"If we did the wrong thing, the fault was mine," Geoffrey interrupted. "I believed at the time we were doing what Master Odo desired. I forbid you to blame our Marshal."

"I'm sorry," Theo apologized. "I don't blame anyone. Certainly not you. It was God's permissive Will."

Geoffrey sat down beside Theo, searching for words which might console. "His Majesty died the way he would have wanted, a brave Crusader in the field and not a leper in a bed. You know it yourself."

Theo nodded. "Yes, I know." He pulled the blanket tighter around him, unable to control his shivering.

"Eat," Geoffrey repeated. "I'm ordering you."

The younger Templar looked at him, and obediently took the charred meat. "We can't leave this place," he announced quietly, "without Dwin's body. He was a king and he deserves a king's burial."

Geoffrey hesitated. He himself felt torn. "None of us wants to leave," he answered. "But we have to get you to Belvoir. The Hospitallers have a fortress there. Your wounds are severe and need proper treatment."

Theo shook his head. "Our King has to be buried with due honor. We owe him that much at least."

Geoffrey sighed.

"Promise me," Theo begged. "Please, Brother Geoffrey."

Geoffrey was silent. He turned his gaze toward the banks of the Jordan River. They'd already spent hours picking through corpses. But he knew his brother would rather die out here of his wounds than leave the King's bones to rot where they lay.

"All right," he promised at last. "We'll search again in the morning. It's too dark now, and you need to get some sleep."

Theo looked at him with gratitude, but then turned away and buried his face in his hands. He still hadn't eaten.

Geoffrey knew that human words were powerless to bring comfort. God alone could ease such crushing grief. Moving closer, he silently put an arm around his brother's shoulders and begged their merciful Father for the strength they both so badly needed.

⮑ Chapter Thirty-One ⮐

SIBYL had spent a lifetime waiting for this day, waiting for the day she would be Queen of Jerusalem. She adjusted the regal robe around her shoulders, tossed her head that her hair might fall just so, and waited for the nervous maidens behind her to pick up the train of her flowing gold-embroidered gown. Then she lifted her chin high and majestically swept forth through the door and toward the dais.

No one, however, bothered to bow. As a matter of fact, the wretches didn't stand up or even seem to notice her!

Sibyl could feel the heat rise to her cheeks. How dare they, the insolent brutes! She shot a look at her husband, already seated in the double throne, but the sight of him only incensed her all the more. Why, the useless milksop couldn't even sit up straight! He was slouched there, his robe all askance, slobbering over a leg of chicken as if this whole affair were nothing but a picnic. Couldn't he behave like a king for ten measly minutes of his life?!

She wondered, with a sharp pang of regret, why she had ever married Guy de Lusignan in the first place. He'd seemed so charming back then, so perfect for her purposes. But now his weaknesses were becoming more apparent with each passing day and he only grated on her nerves. He was still handsome, yes, but so were a hundred other men in the Kingdom.

Well, never mind. It couldn't be helped now. At least he

131

wouldn't stand in the way of her decisions. No, she would reign supreme at his side, and that was all she had ever wanted, really.

But these other men . . . They should be falling over backwards at their Queen's entrance! Yet what were they doing? Just sitting there, actually daring to continue their conversations.

Sibyl reached the front of the room and pierced the group of barons with a poisonous look. But before she could say anything, Guy tossed his drumstick aside and, attempting to stifle a burp, spoke. "Uh, Sib darling. There appears to be a problem in this court."

"So I've noticed!" She climbed up into the huge chair beside her husband and sat down imperiously while the maidens fussed over how best to arrange the long train of her gown. "What's going on here?" she demanded. "Why aren't these men showing due respect?"

"Your cousin, the Count of Tripoli, seems to have some fantastic notion in his head that he has superior claim to our throne," Guy explained. "What do you think about *that?*" To Sibyl's horror, her husband actually laughed. He found it amusing!

Tripoli himself stepped forward, a piece of parchment held triumphantly in his hand. "Your Highness," he addressed her.

"*Majesty!*" she corrected.

He coughed, and Sibyl could see it was only to hide the smirk on his face. "I have here in my possession," he began, "the Last Will and Testament of your brother, the late King Baldwin the Fourth. He had it drawn up shortly after he had received knowledge of your marriage to . . . uh . . . Sir Guy here."

Sibyl froze. She knew nothing about this! She could practically feel the blood draining from her face. "Give it to me!" she shrieked, bolting out of her seat and nearly tripping on her train.

But Tripoli merely drew the parchment against his chest with a flourish and clicked his tongue at her as if she were nothing but a naughty little child.

Sibyl realized he wasn't going to hand it over. She looked at the other barons, then announced, "It's forged."

Tripoli laughed. "Oh, I don't think so. There were plenty of witnesses, so it seems."

She bit her lip and glanced at Guy for support. He only shrugged, obviously as much in the dark as she.

"Read it, my lord," said another member of the court.

The Count unrolled the scroll and cleared his throat. He didn't speak, however. Instead, his eyes scanned the page for the part he was after. Then he looked up. "I'm afraid, Your Highness, that your brother has disinherited you for gross disobedience to his authority. You are no longer in the line of succession for the Throne."

Sibyl's heart stopped.

Next to her, Guy started forward in anger. "*What? Impossible! My wife is the legitimate heiress!*"

"I'm sorry, Sir Guy," Tripoli calmly cut him off. "According to the law of this land, King Baldwin retained the right to choose the man whom his sister would wed and who would thus become his successor. That right was inexcusably violated. His will is a legal document and must be honored as such by this court." The Count tried, but simply could not hide his smile. "As the Princess has been deposed," he went on, "the royal line shall continue through her son, the infant Prince Baldwin, who was born to her by her first husband, the late Prince William Longsword."

A shocked murmur passed through the room, but Tripoli didn't notice, as he delivered his *coup de grace*.

"And as His Majesty is still of the age of minority, I myself claim regency, being the next closest, by blood, to the late King Amalric."

Chapter Thirty-Two

RENAUD de Chatillon, the Hawk of Kerak, held no real hope of taking the Kingship of Jerusalem by force, but, what the heck, it was worth a try. If nothing else, it would be an adventure.

To his way of seeing things, the Throne was simply up for grabs. No one, so it seemed, had the least idea who was supposed to be in charge. Princess Sibyl and her husband were fighting tooth-and-nail to regain their position as legitimate heirs. The Count of Tripoli, on the other hand, was adamant in his assertion that he was *ipso facto* the regent for the child-King Baldwin the Fifth. Others in the court argued that a council of guardianship should be set up until such time as the heir came of an age to rule. The barons of Outremer were fast taking sides, and things in Jerusalem were becoming more and more heated as the days went on. So far no coronation of anyone had taken place.

Thus, it was with as good a chance as any that Kerak rode up to the city walls with his private army of brigands at his rear. Force of arms. That was the easiest way to stake his claim.

It came as no surprise to him, of course, that the gates were locked. He'd been expecting as much. He halted and looked up at the turrets high above. Sure enough, there were Templars up there. They were responsible for protecting the city from predators such as himself.

135

He merely gave them a friendly wave and called out, "Open the gates and let me pass!"

One of the knights came to the edge and leaned over. "I'm sorry, my lord Kerak. We have our orders."

Kerak wasn't perturbed. "Allow me to speak to Gerard de Ridford."

The Templar hesitated, then turned aside to consult with his brothers. There was a brief debate over the issue, but finally two knights disappeared from view and the first came back to the ledge. "Just a minute, my lord," he called down. "The Marshal will be here shortly."

Kerak sat back and waited. He knew exactly how to handle his good friend Gerard.

Within a few moments the Military Commander appeared on the wall. "Ah, Kerak," he greeted. "What a pleasant surprise. I was wondering when you'd show up."

The Hawk shrugged. "Well, why not, Gerard? Why not?"

De Ridford was amused. "I can't let you in, you know."

"Come now. Of course you can."

This was just a little ritual they had to go through and they both knew it.

"State your business here in Jerusalem and I shall consider the matter."

Kerak chuckled. "I've come to be King, of course. What else?"

"Surely that's not all, my friend?"

"I've come also to promise you the position of the next Grand Master of the Order of the Knights of the Temple of Jerusalem." The Hawk grinned. "What do you say, Gerard? May my knights and I join the party?"

De Ridford laughed and turned to the brother beside him. "Open the gates," he ordered, "and let this gentleman and his army in."

∾ Chapter Thirty-Three ∾

SIR Odo de Saint-Amand could hear the iron jangle of keys outside the dungeon door, but he was too weak to sit up. How many days he had been chained here upon this heap of filthy straw he had no way of knowing. The darkness had a way of removing him from time.

The heavy door groaned on its hinges and opened, admitting a shaft of light, and Odo blinked against its brightness. Saladin himself entered the cell, followed by his henchmen, and one of them gave the prisoner a brutal kick in the ribs.

"Get up, vermin!"

Odo clenched his teeth, trying to ignore the pain, and struggled to sit up. The shackles wouldn't permit him to stand.

"What do you want?" he asked.

The Sultan smiled. "You know exactly what I want," he replied. "I desire nothing more than to unchain you and set you free."

"You already know my answer."

"Pity. I thought you would see things my way by now."

The Templar made no reply. He turned his face away.

"All I'm asking is the release of but one of my emirs held captive in King Baldwin's prisons. That's it. Nothing else. Surely a trifling price to pay in order to procure your own freedom."

Odo held his ground. It was against the Holy Rule to be ransomed. "I am a professed religious of Our Lord Jesus Christ, and not some common chattel to be bartered."

An amused smile tugged at the corners of the Sultan's mouth. "Heroic words, Sir Odo. Heroic indeed. But may I remind you that if you refuse my little proposal, you will rot in this dung pit until the day you die?"

The two lords locked eyes for a long moment.

"I realize that perfectly."

Saladin's face hardened. The seconds ticked by.

Finally the Sultan wheeled around and stalked out of the dungeon.

Sir Odo de Saint-Amand let out his breath. Then he closed his eyes to pray.

❧ Chapter Thirty-Four ❧

S IBYL couldn't believe this. She had never once seen her younger half-sister in her entire life, yet here the brat stood, surrounded by a horde of greasy Greek noblemen, actually trying to steal their dead brother's throne.

"In virtue of her relationship to your honorable father, the late King Amalric, Her Highness the Princess Isabella lays claim to the Throne of Jerusalem."

Sibyl stared at the courtier with such venom that the poor fellow backed away a pace or two.

"Remove yourselves and this insolent chit from my palace!" she ordered. "All of you, *out!* This instant!"

Next to her, Guy just couldn't restrain himself any longer. He burst into laughter. "What a circus!" he choked out. "Who will be next?"

Sibyl turned on him like a snake, but the highly amused voice of Sir Humphrey de Toron stopped her. "Well, what do you know?" he asked. "Here comes my stepfather!"

Forty pairs of eyes flew simultaneously to the door as the Lord of Kerak made his triumphal entry into Jerusalem.

Tripoli sprang from his seat. "How did you get in here?!" he demanded.

Kerak flashed him his most charming smile. "Why, the Templars let me in, of course. Who else?"

An angry murmur instantly filled the room and several barons rose, their hands moving to the hilts of their swords.

But Kerak strolled calmly forward and went straight to the dais. "Just thought you'd be interested to know," he informed all present, almost off-handedly, "that I happen to have an army firmly entrenched outside this palace. I'm sure that between them and our dearly beloved monks-of-war, they'll have no trouble convincing you just who the next king should be."

*   *   *   *   *

The Hawk wriggled back into the sumptuously cushioned throne and took a long, leisurely sip from the golden goblet in his hand. He couldn't remember ever having had so much fun in all his born days. How long it would last, he wasn't quite sure, but he was determined to play it for all it was worth.

The rest of the court was in a turmoil, and had been ever since he'd walked in an hour ago. Accusations, insults, bribes flew rampant, as everyone tried to decide how to handle this very awkward situation. He had them all scared stiff, and he knew it. It was one thing for them to deal with his own small private army camped outside these doors, but another thing altogether to deal with Gerard de Ridford's as well!

Whether or not the Templars would really back him in this unbelievably bold venture, Kerak hadn't a clue. But never mind. It was affording him some spectacular entertainment.

He grinned at his stepson, Humphrey de Toron, across the room and shook his head. If only these noblemen could see themselves now, he thought. He never would have believed a group of civilized and cultured men could grow fangs quite so quickly. Sibyl, of course, was worse than any of them. Why his wife, Stephanie, liked her at all he couldn't imagine.

So engrossed was the court in their murderous debate that no one but he noticed when the door opened and four armored knights entered the hall. Their surcoats and mail were filthy, and Kerak's first thought was that fighting had broken out among his men. But then he spotted the figure in their midst.

His heart skipped a beat, and he scrambled out of the throne and off the dais as fast as he could move.

His unexpected leap from the chair and the clatter of his golden goblet as it dropped to the floor startled the others. Bewildered, they followed his gaze, and a gasp went up. Like a rippling wave the barons fell silent, until the only sound was the scuffing of chair legs as all present vacated their seats in haste and confusion.

Then someone recovered enough wits to bow, and instantly every other back bent as well.

Through the stunned silence, the King and his personal guard made their way to the dais and Baldwin took his place, looking more dead than alive. The Templars resumed their usual position, one to each corner of the throne, and for a long moment the King simply sat there, studying the sea of gaping faces before him.

At last he spoke. "So . . . I see you all made it safely back to Jerusalem. May God be thanked."

Tripoli was the first to find his voice. "Sire, we believed you were—I mean, we all greatly feared you had been killed."

"*Hoped*, I daresay would be a more appropriate word," Baldwin corrected. "Perhaps if any of you had bothered to inquire, you would have found you were mistaken."

"To be sure, Sire, naturally we're all overjoyed that

you're back, but how—that is to say, by what wondrous circumstances did you—"

"God never fails to protect those who place their trust in Him, my lord Count, even should His care require a miracle."

No one could think of anything to say. The silence was absolute.

Tripoli searched the room for support. "My dear King," he purred, moving toward the throne. "I assure you—"

There was an unmistakable swoosh and the flash of gleaming steel as four swords were simultaneously unsheathed.

Tripoli froze in his tracks.

The bloodstained Templars showed no emotion, but that meant absolutely nothing. Their very coldness made them all the more threatening.

"I wouldn't advise you, my lord," calmly warned Sir Theodore de Thierceville, "to come any closer."

For the second time in his life, Raymond of Tripoli didn't need to be told twice. He was only too willing to back away. But Baldwin's bodyguards kept their weapons drawn regardless.

No one else dared move.

The King quietly addressed his court. "I may not be able to see much anymore," he told them, "but believe me, I can see straight through the lot of you." He rested his eyes on the blurry figure of the Hawk. "My lord of Kerak, kindly remove your rabble from my courtyard. They are cluttering up valuable space."

Kerak forced a smile. "Of course, Sire. My troops, as always, are entirely at your disposal."

Baldwin refrained from laughing. Instead he turned his attention to his sister. "Sibyl," he said, finding her among the men, "you and your delightful husband may take yourselves back to Jaffa and stay there, where you belong."

Sir Guy glared at Baldwin and opened his mouth to protest, but one look at the Templars was enough to stop him.

Baldwin continued. "As for the rest of you, my loyal and devoted subjects, I have no doubt that, despite my best efforts to prevent it, you will again one day be fighting over the scraps of my Kingdom." Pausing, his gaze slowly swept the gathering, and each person knew he was being judged by his rightful Sovereign. "Next time, however, wait until you have sufficient proof that I am actually dead. As for now, I grant you all my indulgent and, to be frank, most heartfelt leave."

Chapter Thirty-Five

THERE was no need to ask which of the four had sat down beside him at table to help with his evening meal. The King recognized well the individual sounds of their footfalls and knew intimately the varying degrees of roughness each faithful knight used to communicate with him through his failing sense of touch. And he knew without a doubt that this was Brother Bernard.

Ever since their return from that disastrous battle on the Jordan nearly a year ago, Baldwin had stopped taking his meals in the great hall and now dined only in the privacy of his chambers. He could no longer see to feed himself, the disease finally having dug away his eyes. His whole body was dying, piece by piece, and the thought of actually trying to eat in public only filled him with the deepest dread. It was bad enough just having to be seen at all.

"You're not hungry tonight?" Brother Bernard asked gently. Baldwin shook his head. He had no appetite these days.

"You must keep up your strength, Sire."

"For what?" he asked. "That I may live to witness the destruction of my Kingdom?"

"Saladin has agreed to a truce. The fighting has ended for now. You know that."

"The Muslims aren't the only enemies I have."

"I'll take over with this, Brother Bernard," said another voice out of nowhere. "Perhaps you wouldn't mind lighting the fire. His Majesty is freezing."

Baldwin smiled. He hadn't known Theo was there. "Save the wood for the poor," he said. "I'm not cold, honestly."

"Of course you are, Sire. You just don't realize it, that's all."

"Theo, would you stop being such a mother hen all the time?"

There was no answer, but only the sounds of one monk departing and the other sitting down.

"Now eat. I mean it. If only you could see how frail you're becoming."

"I thank God I can't." Baldwin tried to remember the position of the meal set out before him and pushed it away. He heard Theo sigh, and it made him feel guilty. "I'll eat something later," he gave in.

"I'll hold you to it, you know," came the answer. "I don't take lightly a king's word of honor."

Baldwin knew the other three Templars were somewhere out of earshot. Theo only spoke to him so boldly when they were alone. But he was grateful it was just the two of them right now. Sometimes he needed his old friend back, the Theo who was his boyhood companion and not his subject.

He turned his head to where he guessed the other would be and felt a pang of sadness that he would never see his face again. "The barons are right, you know," he said quietly. "I should yield the Throne and just put myself in a lazarhouse somewhere. Surely the Knights of St. Ladre would accept me."

The reply came swift and firm. "No! You've been anointed the true King and no other!"

"But look at me, Theo. Just look at me! I'm a monster. How can my people possibly—"

"Your people love you, Sire! The knights, the peasants, the poor, they all do! You may think they stare at you with loathing, but I can see that trust and deep respect in the eyes of your subjects which you never will."

"You're being kind, and I appreciate it. But you don't have to lie to me, Theo."

"I would never lie to you, Dwin!" The vehemence in Theo's voice startled Baldwin, and he realized the accusation had hurt him. Unthinking, he reached out a hand to his friend, but his skin was so numb that he felt no answering pressure.

"My sister hates me," he continued, "my very own mother is sickened by the sight of me. I can't help but wonder how to make peace with them before I die."

"Not by giving Guy the Throne! For heaven's sake, Dwin, you've already handed him the cities of both Tyre and Jaffa on a silver platter! And in case you haven't noticed, he never even bothered to thank you."

"You don't understand, Theo. This Kingdom is as ravaged by disease as I am. It's dying, it's rotting through, and I'm the one whose job it is to heal it."

"Giving a crown and sceptre to Guy de Lusignan will only hasten its demise, I assure you!"

Baldwin turned away, too weary to fight. The terrible weight of this Kingdom on his shoulders was crushing him.

He drew in a breath and begged God for the grace to be strong, but suddenly even the effort of sitting there seemed beyond him.

Theo saw it, as he always did. "You're tired," he said. "Come on, I'll help you back to bed."

The King only shook his head and asked, "Is there any

news yet from your Grand Master?"

He was talking about Sir Arnold de Torroge, who had been elected to replace Odo de Saint-Amand after the latter had refused to be ransomed and was presumed dead.

"No," said Theo. "He's still in Europe trying to fire up the knights there. But he'll come back soon, and when he does he'll bring a tidal wave of Crusaders with him. You just wait and see. They'll come charging to our rescue by the thousands."

Baldwin couldn't resist a laugh. "Oh, Theo, you're still so innocent sometimes, aren't you? What would I ever do without you?"

"No, it's true, Dwin. The Pope is throwing all his weight behind another Crusade here to Jerusalem. Princes, knights, even kings—they'll all come this time!"

"Europe has grown weary of our holy war. They're too busy fighting other Catholics to care one iota about Saladin. Even if they do eventually show up, I fear it will be too late."

"They've got three years to get here," Theo persisted. "That's plenty of time. Saladin has signed that truce and he won't dare touch us until then."

Baldwin was too exhausted to answer. Trying to rise, he groped for the table edge to use as a support. But his dead hands met absolutely nothing in front of him. Where was the table?

Where was anything?

The whole world was simply disappearing! For a moment he became disoriented and panic threatened to seize him. There was a shattering sound; he realized he must have knocked something over and sent it crashing to the floor.

"Theo," he asked helplessly, "where are you?"

"It's all right, Dwin, I'm here!"

He heard another chair quickly scraping back and then knew his friend had taken hold of him.

Baldwin suddenly felt so humiliated. He didn't want Theo to know just how scared he sometimes was, trapped in this black, unfeeling world and so dependent upon others. He steadied himself and tried to get his bearings.

Then, as always, he did the only thing he could do. He offered his weakness to God and begged for the grace somehow to keep up his role as the brave and fearless King.

ᔥ Chapter Thirty-Six ᔥ

(The Castle of Kerak, 40 miles southeast of Jerusalem)

LADY Stephanie of Kerak had seen that glint in her husband's eye far too many times and knew that it meant trouble. She felt a distinct apprehension steal over her. She knew her husband didn't want her to interfere, but, as usual, she just couldn't help herself.

"Renaud?" she asked, trailing after him into the armory, "why are you wearing your chain mail?"

The Hawk grinned. "To ward off death, of course. Why else, my kitten?"

"But where are you going?"

"Oh, nowhere important. Just outside." He narrowed his eyes and studied the array of swords and battle axes which covered every inch of the wall. At length he selected one and took it down. Stephanie watched as, with loving care, he caressed the razor-sharp edge of the blade with the finger of his steel gauntlet and meticulously blew off a few invisible flecks of dust. Then he stepped back and suddenly whipped the weapon through the air with such unexpected ferocity that his wife gasped and jumped back.

But Kerak only frowned with disappointment. "Useless thing!" he muttered. "Whoever gets away with making toys like this ought to be hung." He replaced it where it belonged and paced the length of the floor, trying to choose another.

Stephanie shuddered. "Uh . . . Hawkie dear?"

"Hmm?"

"There hasn't been a call-to-arms by the King, has there?"

Kerak let out an amused grunt. "Hardly."

She tried again. "Has the truce with Saladin been broken?"

Now he laughed outright. "Not yet, kitten."

"Then why are all your knights mounted in full armor and waiting for you in the courtyard?"

He raised an eyebrow, then winked at her. "Are they now? Well, how terribly convenient." He brought down another weapon, a huge two-handed sword that Stephanie doubted she herself could even lift. But this time she knew what was coming and backed off as far as she could.

Kerak examined the sword closely, then once again slashed it into the empty space as if it weighed but an ounce. He seemed satisfied enough. He quickly moved to the other side of the room to the place where he kept his daggers and slid two into his belt, one on each side. Then, just for safe measure, he took a giant mace off the wall as well. He didn't bother with a shield.

Stephanie loved her Hawkie, but when he got into one of these moods, he scared the living daylights out of her.

"Renaud?" she ventured again.

"Yes, kitten?"

"What are you going to do?"

But in answer to her question he merely came forward, gave her a kiss and said, "Don't bother waiting up. Sleep tight, and sweet dreams."

Then he slammed down the steel visor of his helmet and clanked from the room like some lethal iron machine.

*　　*　　*　　*　　*

Stephanie leaned over the parapet as far as she dared and strained her eyes to see. Next to her, Princess Isabella, the King's half-sister, clutched onto a protruding stone in the wall as if for dear life and stubbornly refused to look down. The sheer drop from the top of the Castle of Kerak to the road far below was giving her an acute attack of vertigo. She had never been so high in her life and wondered how her future mother-in-law could possibly stand there so calmly.

"Don't worry, Issy dear," Stephanie tried to reassure her. "We won't fall, I promise. I've lived here my whole life and I honestly can't recollect falling even once."

The Princess nodded, the absurdity of the statement eluding her, and squeezed her eyes tightly shut. "Are you sure Humphrey will be all right?" she asked, that love-struck tone in her voice which always appeared whenever she spoke of Stephanie's son. She and Humphrey de Toron had met and fallen instantly in love when Isabella had arrived in Jerusalem to stake her unlikely claim to her half-brother's throne.

"Don't you worry about Humphrey. He's a big boy now and can take care of himself."

"Uh . . . what are they doing down there?"

Stephanie craned her neck for a better view. "Well, let's see. By the look of things, I'd say they're hiding behind a hill."

"They can't be hiding very well. I mean, you can see them, can't you?"

"Of course I can. But no one else would be able to."

"Whom exactly are they hiding from?"

"I have no idea in the world."

The Princess bit her lip. "Maybe the castle is under siege."

Now Stephanie turned to stare at her. Didn't the girl

know anything? Or maybe there were no castles in Greece. "We can't be under siege, dear. No one's out there to besiege us. Besides, if we were being attacked, our men would be inside the walls, not out."

Stephanie returned her gaze to the road below, searching for some clue to tell her what her husband was up to.

At last she saw it. A caravan of Arab traders, long and winding, snaking its way across the desert. Even from this distance she could spot the wagons laden high, the camels and mules straining beneath the heavy burdens on their backs. Spices, jewels, perhaps even gold—whatever they were carrying, it was all there for the taking.

And then it hit Stephanie with the force of a battering ram. So *that* was what her husband's army was going to do! The caravan had no choice but to pass along this road, directly below the Castle, and the ambush would all be over before the unsuspecting Muslims even knew what hit them.

She let out a gasp and clapped her hand over her mouth.

But it wasn't just the thought of robbery and murder which made Stephanie's blood run cold. No, she was used to that after so many years with the Hawk. What horrified her was the knowledge that the minute Renaud's knights touched but one of those merchants, the truce with Saladin would be violated, and the Kingdom of Jerusalem would once again be tossed upon the deadly tides of war . . .

⮜ Chapter Thirty-Seven ⮞

(An encampment near Beirut)

THE Hawk of Kerak could not possibly have chosen a worse time to restart the fighting. The Christians of Outremer were already exhausted by too many years of war and were divided amongst themselves. Each petty and hateful faction was ripping the Holy Land into hopeless shreds, and no help had yet arrived from Europe. Baldwin begged Heaven every day to send some strong and holy prince to replace him, someone to whom he himself could surrender his own Kingdom before he died and therefore whose sovereignty could never after be disputed. But if such a prince existed, he had yet to show his face.

A few yards from the King's hastily set up army tent, Guy de Lusignan was nervously pacing inside of his own. He knew this should be his moment of glory—the one chance to regain his wife's claim to the Throne. Baldwin had reluctantly agreed to appoint him Commander-in-Chief of the Army of Jerusalem on the condition that Guy had to prove, once and for all, that he would someday make a worthy king himself. Do that, and Baldwin had promised to put Sibyl back into his will.

Simple. No big deal.

The only problem was, Sir Guy was scared stiff. He hadn't a clue as to what to do first!

His squires were struggling to keep in step with him

153

so that they might fan his face with the long peacock feathers he had insisted they bring along for exactly that purpose. No matter that the rest of the army was ten times hotter than he in their iron coats of mail; that was their problem, not his. He made his way over to the corner, where stood the extravagant four-poster bed which the knights had been forced to drag all the way across the Kingdom, and sat down upon the silken coverlets, burying his face in his hands with despair.

This was a disaster! What on earth was he going to do about all those fearsome troops of Saladin's camped on the opposite side of the valley?

At the entrance of the huge tent, Gerard de Ridford was unable to hide his disgust any longer. He'd been standing there with his group of officers, completely ignored, for over an hour already, and he had finally had enough.

"My lord," he said sharply, "have you arrived at a decision?"

Guy looked up, his eyes blurry from lack of sleep. He didn't seem to understand the question. "Huh?"

"A decision, my lord. We must have one. *Now*."

Guy drew in a deep breath and squared his shoulders. "I am thinking, Sir Gerard. Situations of this nature require deep and profound consideration."

De Ridford and the Templars with him felt nothing but contempt. Sir Guy had been considering deeply and profoundly for days now, and the only results were a diminished food supply and restless, disgruntled troops.

"Situations of this nature," De Ridford retorted, "require but one thing—knights with lances! Let us fight!"

Guy de Lusignan bristled. "*I'm* the one in charge here, De Ridford! I'll decide what my priorities are!"

The Marshal of the Temple cast a look around the luxuriously furnished tent and snorted with derision. "We can all see exactly what your priorities are, my lord." He spun on his heel and started to depart, his honor guard with him.

"And just where do you think you're going?" Guy demanded.

De Ridford turned back to look at him. "To pay my respects to the King," he answered icily. "I find this particular abode too stuffy for my liking."

"I did not grant you leave!"

The Templar scoffed. "I'm taking it anyhow."

* * * * *

In his own sweltering tent, Baldwin lay on the heap of coarse woolen blankets which was all he would allow himself for a bed, consumed though he was with fever and sickness. For a moment he forgot whose voice he had just been listening to. Someone was here to see him, someone important. He fought off the waves of dizziness and tried to remember.

"With all due respect, my lord," Brother Geoffrey was saying from somewhere nearby, "I would strongly suggest you come back later. As you can well see, His Majesty is in no condition to deal with this at present."

"The situation needs resolving! We've all been left in limbo far too long already, and I refuse—"

"Please, my lord," Theo's voice broke in, "it is simply not the right time."

Gerard de Ridford. Of course. That was whom they were trying to get rid of. Their own Marshal.

"Let him stay," Baldwin managed to say. His voice was so weak he wasn't even sure if the others had heard it. But they must have, for the arguing ceased.

"Thank you, Sire. I knew you would agree on the urgency of this matter."

What matter? He couldn't even recall what the Marshal of the Temple had been complaining about. He was so tired.

Think!

Something touched his lips. A cup. He realized one of the Templars was lifting his head, gently pouring a few drops of water into his parched mouth.

"Drink, Sire." Geoffrey's voice.

Baldwin gratefully obeyed. The water was warm and stale, but refreshing nonetheless. Someone else was pressing a wet cloth to his burning forehead.

He heard Sir Gerard heave an exaggerated sigh. "As I was saying, Sire," he continued, "the Sultan has something up his sleeve or he would have attacked us by now. Saladin is not one to dally like this!"

Saladin. Yes, that was it. De Ridford had been telling him about Saladin. And all he wanted to do was sleep!

"What was it you were saying?" Baldwin asked. "I'm sorry. I can't quite remember."

The tone of the Marshal's reply was anything but indulgent, and Baldwin feared this wasn't the first time he had asked his visitor to repeat himself. "The Sultan's army," he answered curtly, "is sitting out there, staring at us."

"I see." *Concentrate!* "And what is Sir Guy doing about it?"

"He's making us sit here and stare back."

Someone else spoke. Brother Bernard. "This is ridiculous! The man can't expect us to wait around here forever playing games with Saladin! Either we fight or we pull back, but he has to decide one way or the other before he has a mutiny on his hands."

Mutiny! A dozen voices seemed to erupt at the word and Baldwin couldn't make out what the men were saying. He realized there were more knights here in his tent than he had thought, and he suddenly remembered that Sir Gerard never went anywhere without his own honor guard of Templar officers.

While they were locked in argument, Baldwin took a few deep breaths and prayed for the strength to deal with all this. Why, he asked himself, had he given Sir Guy command of the situation? Because he couldn't do it himself, that was why, and someone had to be trusted.

He had so much hoped that maybe Sibyl's husband would prove them all wrong, that just maybe Guy de Lusignan had the heart of a king and not that of a coward after all. If only that were true, Baldwin would gladly give his sister back her inheritance and abdicate. But so far his hopes had been in vain.

There was more water, mercifully. He drank.

"Dwin," he heard Theo whisper to him, "just command them to leave. You need to rest."

Baldwin shook his head and ordered himself to concentrate. He knew this was too important to simply dismiss them. "There will be no mutiny," he said as loudly as he could manage. "I'll remove Sir Guy before it comes to anything like that."

The men instantly quieted down.

Sir Gerard spoke. "Then remove him now, Sire! The craven can't even order his own wife around, let alone an entire army! Give me command instead and I'll show those heathen swine what they're just begging to see!"

Baldwin was torn. He knew that De Ridford could no more be trusted than Guy. The Templars were known to err toward the opposite extreme, it was true, but pointless bloodshed and rash military maneuvers weren't the answer either.

He hesitated. De Ridford was far too powerful a man for him to want to offend. In the prolonged absence of Arnold de Torroge, the Grand Master, Sir Gerard was acting as supreme head of the Order in the Holy Land, and the last thing Baldwin needed was for the Templars to turn against him as well!

"Forgive me, my lord," he said carefully, "but I have already entrusted these troops to Sir Guy and I cannot dishonor my word to him."

De Ridford gave a grunt of disgust, but at least he accepted Baldwin's decision. "Sir Guy has never even heard your word of honor, Sire. He has refused to speak to you ever since you deposed his wife."

Baldwin felt a pang. It was true. Neither Guy, Sibyl nor their mother had spoken to him since the contents of his will had been publicly made known. They carried out their business with him through heralds, and even then their messages were always rude and ungrateful.

"Sire, I tell you there's a reason the enemy will not fight," De Ridford persisted. "Saladin must have some plan, some strategy in mind of which we are as yet unaware."

The Marshal's voice was starting to fade again, and Baldwin felt his mind drifting. Everything was becoming unclear, like some black void.

He could vaguely hear Brother Geoffrey telling the others to leave. And then, finally, everything just seemed gently to disappear.

∽ Chapter Thirty-Eight ∾

SIBYL put her hands on her hips and studied her husband across their bedroom with open contempt. How could he actually have done this to her? Their one chance to be reinstated in her brother's will as heirs to the Throne, and Guy had just blown it all to pieces!

He saw the ice in her eyes and responded the only way he knew, by giving vent to his own anger. "How was I supposed to know?!" he bellowed, slamming his fist down hard on the bedside table. "I'm not a mind-reader!"

She didn't react, but Guy winced with the self-inflicted pain and clutched his throbbing hand.

"You let them get away!" Sibyl snapped. "You let Saladin slip through when you should have crushed him!"

"I thought he was retreating! I thought we had scared him senseless and he was—"

"Scared him? *Scared Saladin?* By doing precisely what? Basking in your sunny tents and waving at him for a week? I swear, Guy, you must be the most ignorant toad alive!"

"You weren't there, Sib! You have no idea what was going on!"

She let out a scornful laugh. "Obviously, nothing was going on."

He tried again. "But sweetie, you must believe me. I didn't know he was waiting for us to run out of supplies

159

so that he could turn around and march on Beirut. No one could possibly have guessed!"

"Baldwin guessed!" The words were out before Sibyl realized she had said them. "He was blind and practically dead in that tent, but even *he* figured out what was happening!"

She saw her husband flinch, and she knew the truth hurt him. But his shame only provoked her all the more. "My brother may be a repulsive heap of rot," she continued mercilessly, "but at least he has a brain in his head! Not to mention the courage of a true knight instead of some useless squirming worm!"

"Hey! Are you calling me a—"

"Yes, Guy, I most certainly am!"

For an instant he looked stunned. Then he met her gaze and their eyes locked in a silent battle. It seemed like forever to Sibyl that they stood there glaring at each other, but at last, as she knew he would, Guy lowered his eyes and turned his face away.

She felt like hitting him. She felt like crossing the room and clobbering him to death. What kind of a man was he, that he couldn't even stand up to his own wife!

And then she remembered. It was she herself and no other who had chosen this invertebrate as her husband. She had *wanted* him to be this way! She had actually believed that his weakness would somehow give her power!

Sibyl suddenly wanted to cry with frustration. What a fool she had been to think that she, a woman, could ever be a king! Why hadn't she listened to her brother and saved herself for a real man?

The thought of Baldwin brought a fresh and unexpected stab of regret. Her husband had come home after that disastrous stand-off in the desert, but she had been told exactly where the King had gone. He had had his knights tie him onto his horse and, sick as he was, had ridden at the vanguard of his army all the way to Beirut. Saladin had raised the siege and, as always, God had given her heroic little brother the victory.

And that, the Princess suddenly realized, was the kind of man she wished she'd married.

✎ Chapter Thirty-Nine ✎

THE Lord of Kerak wondered which of the two causes would bring about his death: overeating, or boredom. He knew it had to be one of them.

He glanced around his crowded castle hall and tried to figure out how all of these people could actually keep gorging themselves for an entire week without becoming sick. After all, what was the big deal? A wedding was just a wedding—people got married all the time—and why he should be the one to finance the stuffing of so many faces for day after tedious day was beyond his understanding.

Still, he thought with a sigh, if this was what made his little Kitten happy, then he'd just put up with it for a bit longer. Their son Humphrey had finally married the Princess Isabella, and Stephanie was determined to make this the most regal and magnificent celebration the Kingdom had ever seen. Well, he had to hand it to her. He never would have imagined she could get so many important personages to show up.

As a matter of fact, apart from the religious there were only two significant persons in the realm who seemed to be missing. One was Guy de Lusignan. Princess Sibyl had claimed he was tied up in Jaffa and couldn't get away, but everyone guessed the truth, of course. She just didn't want him here spoiling her fun.

The second guest who had humbly declined their invitation was none other than the King himself. He, by all accounts, was simply too busy dying to bother coming all this way for a party.

Kerak set his empty goblet down on a page's tray and slipped out of the noisy hall. Dusk was falling, and the evening air would be fresh and cool. That's what he needed right now, a bit of breathing space.

He climbed the winding stairs to the turrets and stepped outside. He didn't feel comfortable leaving his castle unguarded like this, even for a few short hours, but Stephanie had been so insistent that the watchmen should all join in the festivities. So, being the indulgent husband that he was on occasions like this, he had let his Kitten have her way.

But the minute Kerak's gaze fell upon the road far below, he gave a start, then froze with disbelief.

This was impossible! Absolutely impossible!

For a long moment he could do nothing but stare at the fearsome sight. Then he recovered the use of his limbs, whipped around and raced back down the stairs to sound the alarm.

∞ Chapter Forty ∞

PRINCESS Sibyl was becoming scared. Genuinely scared. Kerak's fortress had been under siege for days now, and she knew exactly why the Sultan had brought his army here. Just about every notable fighting man in the Kingdom, excluding the warrior monks, was holed up inside these walls, and someone—some traitor—had told Saladin that they would be. He had only to take the Castle of Kerak, and Jerusalem would be wide open.

Sibyl paced the floor of her room alone and tried to think. All of the other ladies were huddled together in the chapel, begging Heaven for help, while the men were out there on the walls fighting for their lives. As for herself, the Princess had never before felt so utterly at the mercy of others.

The noises outside her window were appalling! She hadn't realized just how frightful a battle could sound. So many screams of agony, so many thousands of arrows whizzing through the air—bangs and crashes and such cacophony that listening to it all made her shudder. She had always imagined that, if she were the Queen, she would don a coat of mail and fight as bravely as any knight. But now she understood that she had no place in this violent world of men, nor did she want one! All she wanted was to get out of this nightmare alive!

There was a sudden rap on her door, and despite herself she jumped. With all the racket outside she was half expecting the ceiling to cave in on her at any minute, or the floor to crumble away beneath her feet.

She tried to steady her racing heart and compose herself like a princess. "Yes?" she called out, hearing her voice sound just a bit too loud. "You may enter."

The door opened and Lady Stephanie came in, followed by a couple of dashing young squires. Sibyl was astonished at how calm her cousin managed to look, as if bloodshed were a perfectly normal part of her daily life. But, of course. Stephanie was married to the Hawk.

"Sib dear," she said, "don't look so worried. These two brave young men have volunteered to attempt an escape. They think they can break out of the castle through the gardorobe and get a message to your husband."

"My husband?" Sibyl asked blankly. "Why my husband?"

"Because he's our only hope. If he moves quickly enough, he might be able to organize some kind of resistance and come to our rescue."

The Princess couldn't believe her ears. Guy, come to the rescue of the Kingdom? *Never!*

She didn't hesitate an instant, but turned to the squires and took charge. "Forget my husband," she commanded. "If you can sneak out of here, go straight to Jerusalem and get my brother. He'll save us!"

"Sib!" Stephanie gasped. "You can't be serious! The King is dying."

The Princess squared her shoulders and replied with complete confidence: "Baldwin has been dying for years. He'll come anyway. You just wait and see!"

✐ Chapter Forty-One ✐

BROTHER Geoffrey wasn't sure whether the King was asleep or merely resting. It was so difficult to tell these days, ever since the disease had so cruelly taken away his eyes. But even if he was awake, Geoffrey hated the thought of having to do this to him. As if the dying young Monarch didn't already have enough to bear without this news on top of it all!

He had left the two squires in the antechamber, where several pages were attending to their refreshment, and had returned to the King's bedroom. Brother Bernard was the only other one there, kneeling at the prie-dieu in the corner, reciting his Office. Brothers Theo and Marcel had gone down to the Temple yard, as they all must, for their daily practice in arms.

Geoffrey approached the bed and asked hesitantly, "Sire?"

"It's all right," Baldwin assured him with a weak smile. "I'm not asleep. Who is it?"

"Brother Geoffrey." He realized with a pang of sadness that the King could no longer distinguish between their voices. Going closer, he sat down on the edge of the mattress and took one of the leper's hands. He gave it a hard squeeze. He knew Baldwin's nerves were so damaged now that he couldn't feel any pressure, but Geoffrey wanted to make some kind of contact before dealing this terrible blow. "Sire," he said gently, "there's an urgent

166

message from the Castle of Kerak. Two of his squires are
here to see you."

The King gave a nod, and Geoffrey knew it was a nod
of resignation to yet another cross. "Yes, of course," he
answered. "If you would be so kind as to help me get
ready, then you can show them in."

Baldwin found it mortifying to have to give audience to
those who had never met him. He had never decided
whether being unable to see their reaction made the
ordeal easier to bear or only the more humiliating. But
his knights seemed to understand this, and they always
made sure these days that his face was covered.

He was unable to stand anymore, his feet as dead now
as his other limbs, but his team of bodyguards realized
that as well. Geoffrey stood up and took him in his arms.
Baldwin was so wasted and thin that it was like lifting a
child, and the Templar easily carried him to his chair.
Then he made sure the King was as comfortable as could
be hoped for, and carefully shrouded his face.

"Brother Geoffrey?"

"Yes, Sire?"

"Do you know their message?"

Geoffrey hated this. Why did he have to be the one to
add more weight to a burden already so crushing? Yet
better he than Brother Theo. He knew his youngest
brother felt the pain of all this more than any of them.
And judging by the way he himself was feeling, that was
a lot.

"Yes, Sire, I know the message," he admitted reluctantly. "The fortress of Kerak is under attack. If Saladin
can take it—and it looks as if he will unless reinforcements are sent—then it's not hard to guess where his
next stop will be."

From beneath the veil of material came a soft moan,

then the King bowed his head. Geoffrey, too, said a silent prayer for the courage he knew poor Baldwin needed.

After a moment the faceless figure spoke, and his voice, as usual, was not only resigned, but calm. Geoffrey marveled at how one with so little life left in him could always remain so brave and strong. "God will help us, Brother Geoffrey," Baldwin said. "We just have to keep trusting in Him."

"Sire, what would you like me to do?"

"Bring Kerak's squires in to see me, then send messages to both Sir Gerard and the Master of the Knights of Saint John."

"What shall the messages say, Sire?"

To Geoffrey's amazement, Baldwin actually managed to sound lighthearted. "Tell them I want every Templar and every Hospitaller they can muster. The monks have all just been issued a royal invitation to the most spectacular wedding party this Kingdom has ever seen!"

∾ Chapter Forty-Two ∾

THERE was so much noise. Baldwin tried to sort through it all to decide which of the sounds were real. It was becoming almost impossible to discern these days. No doubt most of the chaotic din truly came from the distant battle, but all of that strange buzzing, he suspected, existed only in his own ears.

He'd been trying hard to ignore it for months now, and he didn't know how he was ever going to bear it bravely, but deep in his heart Baldwin had to admit the truth. Along with everything else, he was going deaf.

He asked of God every day to take him before it happened completely. The thought of living in a black and silent void, with no sensation in his limbs and no ability to care for himself, was terrifying. Sound was the last thing that kept him in touch with reality, and once that was gone, his whole world and everyone in it would simply vanish.

Yet if God willed even that, Baldwin would accept it with trust.

He felt that familiar fear grip him and fought it back with a prayer. Instead, he tried to draw his thoughts to the present, and was suddenly ashamed to be dwelling on his own miseries when so many courageous Crusaders were out there shedding their blood in God's cause.

He tried to visualize where he was and what was

happening. He knew he was somewhere outside of Kerak's castle, propped up in a litter because his guards had actually refused this time to put him on a horse. Even more, they'd been adamant that he travel in the center of the Templar army, surrounded by hundreds of monks and thus protected on every side, instead of carrying him in the front line where he had always ridden since his very first battle at the age of thirteen.

As for now, Baldwin knew he'd been left behind in the care of several trusted sergeants, although he wasn't sure exactly how many. There hadn't been any question this time about whether or not his own four would fight. The survival of the Kingdom depended on this battle, and every single knight he'd brought with him was needed.

"*Deus le vult!* God wills it! God wills it!" Through all the clamor in the distance he suddenly heard the battle cry ring out, loud and strong, and he knew his Kingdom still lived.

Baldwin bowed his head and begged the Almighty that it would not die.

*   *   *   *   *

Theo could tell from the angle of the arrows that they were pouring down from the turrets of Kerak Castle. The Crusaders up there were actually shooting at them. It took a moment or two before he realized that this was a good sign. It meant the Templar line had cleaved through the besieging Muslims all the way to the foot of the fortress, but the barons behind those great walls had not yet spotted it amidst the chaos.

Saladin's men were fast thinning out, sandwiched as they were between the two Christian forces; and even as he fought with all his might, Theo knew the victory was already theirs. The Kingdom of Jerusalem could not so easily be vanquished. No, it simply refused to die so long as Baldwin remained upon that Throne.

Somewhere far behind him he faintly heard the Crusaders' battle cry and realized that another wave of knights had been sent into the melee. Hospitallers, most likely. All of his own brothers were already in the thick of it.

No sooner had that cry died out than it was taken up by others, louder and much closer this time. Through the surging sea of horsemen and bloody weapons, Theo saw just what they had been waiting so long to see. The castle gates were at last thrown open, after weeks of siege, and a torrent of Christian warriors flooded forth to finish cutting down the enemies of Christ.

* * * * *

"Both of you," Brother Geoffrey ordered, "get over here and hold him down!"

Brother Bernard pulled off his steel gauntlets. He had just ridden over to join the other three, but straightaway he could see what he was going to have to do, and he was already dreading it. Reluctantly he swung down from his saddle. He detested this sort of thing.

"Brother Geoffrey?" the King asked beside them. "What are you going to do to him?"

Geoffrey hesitated. "Don't worry about it, Sire." He attempted to wipe the sweat from his eyes so that he could see better, and Bernard noticed how white his face was beneath the dark streaks of red.

Beside his own horse, Marcel was stripped of most of his chain mail. His wounds had already been bound, but his tunic was saturated with blood. He looked dizzy and slightly sick, and Bernard wondered if he were about to pass out. But he wasn't allowed to. Not just yet, anyway. First he had to help with this.

"Is it an arrow?" Baldwin asked. No one contradicted him, so he knew he was right. Instinctively he tried to get up. "How bad is it?"

"Not too bad," Theo managed to answer. "Honestly. I hardly feel a thing."

But the others could see that the arrow was deeply embedded and must be killing him. Geoffrey wasn't sure yet how he was even going to get the thing out. He had already cut away the side of Theo's hauberk, but that was as far as he'd gotten.

"Where is it?" Baldwin asked. He felt so useless!

"Nowhere vital," Brother Geoffrey assured him. "Just in the ribs. He'll be fine." He turned to the other two knights and ordered again, "Get over here and hold him down!"

Instantly Brothers Bernard and Marcel moved. They went forward and knelt on the ground beside their youngest brother. He cast them both a pleading look but didn't resist when they locked him in vice-like grips and held him still.

Bernard wondered if Theo realized just how excruciating this was going to be. The pain of an arrow being driven in was one thing; the agony of having it ripped back out was entirely another. Even the toughest of knights found this particular ordeal almost unbearable.

"We won, Theo," Baldwin said softly. "You saved the Kingdom. All of you did, by the mercy of God. Just like at Ascalon."

The monks knew he was trying to distract Theo, and they were grateful. Brother Geoffrey took a firm grasp on the shaft. He wished he wasn't the one who had to do this!

"After all this time," the King continued, "and do you realize I still don't know? Does Saladin really have six eyes and horns on his head?"

Amazingly, Theo laughed. "Actually, Sire," he managed to answer, "it's seven. And his tail is purple with little pink—" Geoffrey yanked on the arrow.

It was all the other two could do to hold their brother down, yet to their astonishment he didn't cry out as the thing was wrenched back out through the entry wound, followed by a pulsing jet of blood. It was like pulling out a cork. Geoffrey quickly clamped a hand over the pumping hole while he examined the shaft.

He winced. The head was missing.

Bernard and Marcel looked at each other in dismay. They knew, even before Geoffrey unsheathed his dagger, that he was going to have to dig the thing out. Feeling like a pair of fiends, they tightened their already brutal grips and kept their victim down.

"Just keep being brave, little brother," Geoffrey said. "I'll get this over with as quickly as I can, I promise."

Deathly pale, Theo could only nod.

On impulse, Baldwin reached out in the direction of their voices, wanting so much to help. Theo saw, and gratefully grabbed his hand. So tightly did Theo hold on that, to Baldwin's surprise, he could actually feel the pressure from that anguished grip. It had been so long since he had felt anything! He thanked God that he was able to give this small measure of comfort to his friend, and for the briefest of moments the leper King felt more alive than he had for years.

He heard Theo let out a pained gasp as Geoffrey sliced him open, but to the edification of them all, the young monk gave no more indication of his agony. Instead, withdrawing into himself, he began to murmur, "Thy will be done; not mine, O God, only Thine . . ."

❧ Chapter Forty-Three ❧

THEO had been a Templar for nearly eight years now, and of those eight, six and a half had been spent in the continual presence of his King and these three, now his closest brothers.

He couldn't help but wonder how he was going to adjust to living among strangers in another house of the Order. He knew, though, that it would only be a matter of weeks before his services were no longer needed here in the Royal Palace. Soon these rooms would be occupied by a different Baldwin, Sibyl's little son, who remained heir to the Throne.

Sir Gerard de Ridford, their Grand Master since the recent death in Europe of Sir Arnold de Torroge, had already informed the four bodyguards of their next postings. Brothers Marcel and Bernard would be going back to Gaza after all these years. Brother Geoffrey had been elected to replace one of the officers who had died at the siege of the Castle Kerak and would remain here in Jerusalem. As for himself, Theo was being sent to the northernmost regions of the Kingdom, to a garrison he'd never even heard of.

His only consolation was the thought, *God wills it*.

He didn't let himself think about the day when he would have to kneel at the feet of a new Sovereign and swear the Oath of Fealty. His whole life he had wanted to be a Knight Templar, but somehow he had always been so sure that Dwin and no other would be the King he served. Yet in a few weeks the regency would pass to Count Raymond of Tripoli until such a time as Baldwin the Fifth came of an age to rule.

The little Prince, however, had always been sickly, and was not expected to live long. Who would ascend the Throne after him, Theo wasn't sure. What he was sure of, though, was that the Kingdom of Jerusalem was dying right alongside its brave and faithful Monarch.

It tore Theo's heart to have to stand here at the foot of the bed like some lifeless sculpture and keep vigil while so many people came and went. It made him feel as if his friend were already in a coffin. But Dwin was a King, and this was what knights must do when their King was dying. Stand here immobile, clasping their sword hilts and keeping their faces expressionless.

Across from him, at the head of the bed, Brother Marcel was doing the same. How many days and nights the four of them had been taking turns at this, Theo had lost count. It wasn't so bad when Dwin was awake. Then at least, if no one else was there, they could sit beside him and try to help. But when he slept, as he did now, Theo was always afraid he would simply never wake up again.

Most of the Kingdom had already come to say good-bye. Not just the nobles and knights, either. The peasants, the sick and poor, the lowliest of subjects had streamed to the Holy City to pay their homage to the ruler they so loved and respected. And Dwin, of course, had received them all, no matter how exhausted he had been or how much the effort had cost him. The only ones who had not come were the members of his own family, and hard as Baldwin tried to hide it, Theo knew it pained him deeply.

A priest had administered the Last Sacraments, but to Baldwin's great sorrow he was no longer able to receive

Holy Communion. The disease had done its cruel damage to his mouth and tongue as well, and it was nearly impossible for his knights to get any food into him at all.

Theo silently began to recite the prayers for the dying, as he had done so many times in these last few weeks. It would actually be a relief, he thought, when all this was finally over.

Across the room he heard the door open, and there were a few quiet voices. He ignored them. The chamberlain was constantly ushering people in and out these days, and it was no concern of his. His job was simply to stand here and look strong when he didn't feel it.

"Brother Theodore?" one of the voices called out.

He looked over and saw two sergeants from the Temple. They obviously had a message for him. He left his place at the foot of Baldwin's bed, and Brother Bernard immediately crossed the room to replace him.

"What is it?" he asked when he had reached them.

"Master Gerard wants you to come down to the Temple. You have a visitor there."

"A visitor? Who?"

The sergeants exchanged a look, and Theo could see they found some sort of private joke in their announcement.

"It's Her Most Royal and Imperious Highness, the gorgeous Princess Sibyl herself," one of them told him, then added with a wink, "you lucky dog."

Well, they might find it amusing, but Theo certainly didn't. "Who let her into the monastery?" he demanded. "Women are absolutely forbidden to—"

"Look, don't blame us, Brother! We're just the lowly knaves who lick the boots of knights like you. If you have a bone to pick, then pick it with De Ridford."

Theo bristled. "We're not allowed to hold conversation

with women. It's against the Rule. Master Gerard knows that full well." He turned to go back to his post, but one of the sergeants roughly grabbed his arm and restrained him.

"You've been given a direct order, Brother."

Theo couldn't believe this. He looked at the sergeant's hand for a moment, then jerked his arm free. His eyes searched the room for Brother Geoffrey.

The other knight saw and came over. "Is there a problem here, Brothers?" he asked.

"No."

"Yes," Theo answered. "I've been commanded to see the Princess. In our monastery."

Geoffrey frowned. "By whose orders?"

"Guess."

There was a short silence and Theo knew his brother was fuming as well. Finally Geoffrey said, "Go with them. I'm afraid you have no choice."

"I want you to accompany me."

Geoffrey glanced back at the bed to see that the King was still peacefully asleep. Then he nodded and replied, "All right. I'll come."

* * * * *

Sibyl wrung her hands and shifted uneasily on the hard wooden bench. She wished Theo would hurry up so she could get this ordeal over with. This place unnerved her. It was no different from a thousand other rooms she had been in before, but somehow it seemed so austere, so forbidding, and she didn't like it. Maybe it was because no other female had set foot in here for nearly a hundred years, and she sensed she did not belong.

It amazed her how easily Gerard de Ridford had admitted her into the Temple. Surely Sir Odo, had he still been alive, would never have permitted such a violation, even at the request of the Royal Princess herself. But the new Grand Master obviously had no such scruples and had even gone so far as to say she could speak with Theo alone.

Sibyl realized that she was nervous, and it annoyed her. There was no earthly reason why she should be. After all, she'd known Theo ever since they'd been children, when he was nothing but a menial page in her father's household and had worshipped the very ground she'd walked on, as had every boy at court.

Or . . . had he? To be perfectly honest, Sibyl had never been completely sure.

Nor was she so sure he would agree to do what she was about to ask of him now. Any other man would, of course. No male in his right mind had ever been able to resist her charm, and getting her way had always been child's play. Yet this time, Sibyl knew, the stakes of her game were high. Very high, and it all hinged on Theo's cooperation!

The door finally opened and, to her dismay, Sibyl saw that Theo had not come alone. A second Templar entered with him, one she recognized only as another of Baldwin's bodyguards. The two were clothed not in mail but in the seemingly innocent monastic habits of their Order. Nonetheless, Sibyl could discern their swords beneath the folds of white material and knew that, as always, her brother's guards were fully armed.

The pair stopped just inside the door. Neither made a move to close it. Then, inevitably, they took up the usual Templar stance, side by side, and kept their eyes lowered as if even the sight of a beautiful woman was sinful.

Sibyl was irked. She knew their Rule forbade them to look upon her, but she so much wanted Theo to be a bit more human right now, not some impassive statue!

"Your Highness," Theodore greeted her. "You requested to see me."

His brother remained silent.

It had been years since Sibyl had actually spoken to Theo, and she couldn't decide whether or not she should rise. It made her feel more majestic, of course, to be seated while they stood, but perhaps that wasn't the best tactic just now.

She rose to her feet. "Thank you for coming, Theo. I—"

The other monk raised his eyes and shot her a look. Sibyl instantly realized her mistake. Flustered, she began again. "Brother Theodore, I wanted to . . . well, I . . ." She stopped. She wished the other Templar would just leave! He was making her nervous standing there like that. This conversation was none of his business! She plopped back down on the bench and haughtily ordered, "Leave us, Sir Knight! I wish to speak to your brother alone."

"I'm sorry, Your Highness," he answered, "our Holy Rule will not allow it."

"This meeting is already enough of a violation," Theo said. "Whatever you have to say to me may be said in the presence of my brother."

"I've violated nothing! Your Grand Master himself gave you a dispensation to talk to me in private."

The hardness on both their faces showed her exactly what they thought of Sir Gerard's dispensations.

"That may be so," Theo replied, "but I've granted no such permission to myself."

Sibyl felt her cheeks grow hot and realized then that Theo had no respect for her. For some reason the knowledge stung. She wanted a man like him to consider her a lady.

She directed a hostile glare at the other knight, but his eyes were again locked on the floor and he either didn't notice or, more likely, simply didn't care. Either way, she knew he wasn't going to leave. She had no choice but to ignore the brute.

Taking a deep breath, she plastered her sweetest expression onto her face and tried to decide how to begin again. "How is . . . I mean . . . is my dear brother faring any better?" she asked tentatively.

"No, my lady," Theo told her. "He is extremely weak. He'll not recover this time, but he bears it bravely."

Sibyl bit her lip and thought it might be a good idea to stand back up. She had to get Theo to agree to her plan. It was her last chance!

"I've asked you to come here," she said, "because I need your help. You've always been closer to Baldwin than anyone else in the world, and if there's one person he'll listen to, it's you."

Now Theo actually raised his eyes. It was only for an instant, but that was all it took. "Should Your Ladyship be in any way hinting that I try to get him to change his will on your behalf, then all I can say is I'm sorry but—"

"That's not it!" she blurted. *The pious toad! How had he guessed?!*

Theo fell silent and stood there, waiting.

Sibyl made a snap decision. The old damsel-in-distress-routine. That was the best way to manipulate men like Theo. Appeal to their chivalry.

She put on a face of dove-like innocence and fluttered her eyelids, blinking back imaginary tears. What man could possibly resist when she gazed at him so trustingly like this?

But, to her frustration, Theo stubbornly kept his eyes on the floor. Sibyl found herself hating the monastic Rule which stripped men like him of their hearts and made them about as susceptible to passion as a lump of clay!

What a tragic waste of manhood! And to think . . . she could have made him a King!

Regret stabbed her, so sharp it was almost physical, and it was with an effort that Sibyl brought her attention back to the role she was trying to play.

"I've done something wrong," she whispered in her most angelic tone, forcing her voice to tremble. "Terribly, terribly wrong, and I need forgiveness."

"There are many priests available to grant you such, my lady," Theo replied. "I, alas, am not one of them. May we now withdraw?"

This wasn't working! "Please, Theo! You don't understand!" Sibyl instinctively reached out to touch his arm, but he drew back as if she were a deadly poison.

"What actually is it, Your Highness," he asked, "that you want of me?"

The mere fact that he bothered to ask indicated to Sibyl that maybe he still had a heart after all. If she played her part carefully, she just might be able to dupe him yet.

"I want you to tell Baldwin that I'm . . . simply that I'm so very sorry." The words threatened to choke her. "I've treated my brother so badly all these years; I know that now. Ask him to forgive me, Theo, before he dies. Please." She shot a quick look at the other Templar and felt the resentment burning in her. She wished so much he wasn't listening to this, even if he was just another lump of clay. It was bad enough having to grovel in front of one man, let alone two! Yet if this was the price she had to pay to be reinstated as the King's heiress, then she would just have to endure it.

Theo was silent for a long moment, and she felt a glimmer of hope. He was considering her request, possibly he even believed her. And if he believed her, then Baldwin would surely believe him. Sibyl held her breath, awaiting his answer.

Finally he asked, "Might it not be better if you came with us and spoke to him yourself? You don't know how much it would mean to him, my lady."

The Princess had been so afraid Theo would say something like that. It would be a test of her sincerity. But the very thought of entering that contaminated chamber sent a shudder through her. One could hardly beg forgiveness from the doorway! She would actually have to touch Baldwin and . . . she'd rather die! It would be so much easier to get Theo to do it for her.

"I can't go in there," she objected. "Baldwin will refuse to speak to me. I know he will. He hates me."

"That's not true, Your Highness. Dwin couldn't harbor hatred in his heart if he tried. You must believe me."

Sibyl was unable to think of anything to say. How could Theo be so cruel as to expect a lady of her rank and bearing to expose herself to such a dreadful disease? This wasn't just any old illness, after all. This was leprosy!

The silence began to stretch and, for the second time, Theo looked up. Sibyl knew he was trying to read her heart through her eyes, and she felt suddenly vulnerable.

After what seemed to her an eternity, he sadly shook his head and said, "If you seek forgiveness, which both Our Lord Jesus Christ and your brother the King are certainly willing to grant you, then I'm afraid you must ask for it yourself."

He looked then at his brother, who, Sibyl saw, gave him an almost imperceptible nod of approval. Without another word, the two Templars turned and departed, taking with them Sibyl's last hope of becoming Queen.

∽ Chapter Forty-Four ∽

APART from the royal physicians and Baldwin's own confessor, the Templars no longer let anyone into the room. They saw no reason for others to enter these days, as their King was now both blind and deaf, and they wanted him to be able to die in peace. All of his subjects who had desired to say good-bye had already had their chance, and as far as the affairs of government were concerned, Count Raymond of Tripoli had assumed regency until such a time as the little heir would attain his majority. Baldwin, wisely, had realized that the only way to prevent his cousin Tripoli from aiding Saladin was to allow him the power he craved, thus ensuring that he would fight against the Muslims instead of with them. It was, alas, a small guarantee of keeping the Kingdom in Christian hands, but it was the best Baldwin could do.

Now only one job remained for the dying Monarch—that of preparing his own soul for its entrance into eternity.

Brothers Geoffrey and Marcel were sitting beside him, as they had been for the past several hours, and they could tell by their King's labored breathing that the end was indeed very near. They both knew Baldwin must be parched with thirst, for his fever burned high, yet his mouth was so ulcerated that it was impossible for him to swallow the water which Geoffrey had been trying so patiently to give him all this time. He suspected that poor Baldwin didn't even realize the cup was there at all.

At last Geoffrey gave up and turned to Brother Marcel. "I think you'd better go wake our brothers," he said.

Marcel nodded, understanding, and crossed the room to where the four Templars themselves slept these days, in order to be closer to the King. Geoffrey had hesitated to disrupt his two brothers' sleep, for he knew they were exhausted. Theo, especially, had hardly taken any rest or food for days. Yet Geoffrey also knew the hour had finally come.

He reached once again under Baldwin's collar and pressed his fingers against his pulse. It was very slow now, so weak that he could just barely feel it.

He realized it was time to tell the chamberlain that the prayers of the city were needed.

*   *   *   *   *

The buzzing in Baldwin's ears had stopped a few days ago, and as a result all other sounds had likewise ceased. His world was now totally silent and dark. Baldwin felt as if his lungs were collapsing, and every breath caused pain. But what was torturing him most of all was the unbearable thirst. He couldn't help but wonder why his friends were leaving him like this, with nothing to drink, for so long. Nor had there been any food for what he was sure must be days, and the emptiness in his stomach was unlike anything he had ever suffered before.

He knew his Templars must be there, somewhere, though he could no longer prove to himself their presence. But he refused to believe they had abandoned him. No, they would never do that, surely! Yet even so, Baldwin had a hard time, these last few days, convincing himself that anyone was there at all.

This thirst was an agony! Didn't they realize? *Why wouldn't they help him?*

He had never known how hard this was going to be, to die with no human comfort and assailed by so many fears. He tried to pray, to abandon himself to God's loving mercy, but he was scared. Scared to face the Eternal King in all His infinite justice when that hour would soon come. To render an account for each and every one of his personal failings was frightening enough, but to answer for his keeping of the entire Kingdom was overwhelming, and Baldwin had never been so terrified before.

How severe, he knew, must be the Judgment of kings! How many souls, how many decisions, he would have to answer for! The weight of it all was crushing! If only someone could lighten the burden, could reassure him in his fears.

"Theo?" he gasped.

The effort to speak was so great that he didn't even know whether his voice could be heard. He waited, hoping against hope for a sign that his friend was there. Just to feel some slight pressure, to hear some faint sound in that silent void, would make such a difference right now!

But . . . there was nothing.

He drew in a last rasping breath and tried again. "Theo? Are you there?"

Still, nothing.

He was alone.

King Baldwin offered this final anguish to God, and silently begged for His mercy.

*   *   *   *   *

Theo hadn't realized he had fallen into such a deep sleep, and even though Brother Geoffrey had ordered him to take some rest against his own will, he still felt ashamed that he had been lying there, actually *sleeping*, and all the while Dwin had been facing death.

He stumbled to his feet, inwardly acknowledging his human incapacity to help. The closest friend he had ever had in all his twenty-five years was about to die, and he wouldn't be able to let poor Dwin know that he was even there.

Only prayer remained.

As he hastily pulled on his mantle, he saw that Marcel was waking Brother Bernard as well. Silently, he began reciting the Prayers for the Dying, and although the words had long since been memorized, Theo doubted that he had ever said them with quite the same fervor as he did now. Then together the three monks crossed the room and knelt next to their oldest brother at the King's bedside.

Geoffrey looked up, and Theo noticed that his cheeks were streaked with tears. Seeing him like that made it all the harder to bear. "He's been asking for you," Geoffrey said. "I don't think he realizes that any of us are here."

Theo rose from his knees, and the others moved aside so that he could sit on the edge of the bed. "Dwin," he whispered, taking the dying King in his arms, "we're here. We're all right here with you."

He knew, of course, that his words would not be heard, but it helped to say them anyhow.

Far in the distance a church bell began to toll, followed soon by others, and Theo knew that the city was being asked to pray for the passage of their King's soul into eternity. He felt his own tears welling up inside him, and for once didn't even try to hold them back.

Together the four monks prayed, and waited for the end.

∽ Chapter Forty-Five ∾

THE Solemn Requiem Mass was to be offered tomorrow in the Church of the Holy Sepulchre. The King would be buried there, close to the spot where the Precious Body of Christ had been laid to rest and had later risen so gloriously from the dead. Brother Geoffrey had always loved and revered this place more than any other, but now it was to become doubly special to him.

As he stood there, motionless, keeping vigil at the coffin along with three Jerusalem Templars whose names he didn't even know, he couldn't help but wonder how long this church would remain in Christian hands. Countless thousands of lives and almost a hundred years of bloodshed had been the price the Crusaders had paid to guard this, the holiest spot on the face of the earth. And yet, he thought to himself, it had probably all been in vain. The glory of God was no longer what drove the Christian barons of Outremer to fight against the Infidel, and Geoffrey knew that any lesser motive could not possibly draw down the blessings of Heaven upon their war. Even his own Order was now so riddled with corruption that it must be displeasing to God Almighty. That alone was enough cause for sorrow.

He had been standing here for hours, and soon other Templars would come to relieve him. But none of them

would feel the pain in the same way he did. Master
Gerard de Ridford had seen no reason why Brothers
Marcel and Bernard should stay for the funeral when the
Gaza Chapter was already so short of knights, and they
had been ordered to leave. Geoffrey knew that Brother
Theo also, accompanied by two sergeants, must depart
north to his new assignment this very morning. Whether
or not he would ever see any of them again, Geoffrey had
no idea, and the thought stung.

Behind him he heard the church doors suddenly flung
open. There were voices, a commotion of some kind, and
the sound of a woman sobbing. Geoffrey kept his eyes on
the coffin, on all those flickering candles, and tried to dis-
regard the noise. Then there was a rush of footsteps echo-
ing in the vast space, and a lady in black appeared and
threw herself down on her knees before the coffin.

Geoffrey found it strange that, before bowing her head,
she swiftly looked around to assure herself that all those
present were watching. He didn't realize who she was
until Guy de Lusignan strode up after her and roughly
grabbed her by the arm.

"Sib, stop it!" he hissed. "You're making a spectacle of
yourself! Get up and behave like a princess!"

She wrenched her arm free and buried her face in the
folds of the black cloth draped over the coffin, her shoulders heaving with seemingly uncontrollable sobs.

Geoffrey knew it was beneath him, but somehow he
could find little sympathy in his heart for the woman
who had jeopardized her brother's Kingdom and had
caused Baldwin his greatest sorrow. She might weep like
a Magdalen now, when the box was sealed and the disease safely contained within it, but he strongly suspected
it was nothing but a show.

He said a silent prayer to fight against the anger

inside him, and tried to ignore her.

Sir Guy, frustrated, once more gave up his attempt at manhood and stalked off in a huff, sweeping past three Templars who had just entered and were making their way toward the coffin. Two were sergeants, only one a knight and in full mail, which they always had to wear when they traveled.

They spotted Sibyl, and the sergeants hesitated to approach, no doubt unwilling to intrude upon such heart-rending grief. They knelt down where they were, but the knight went forward alone to the King's casket. Geoffrey had no need to look in order to know who the mail-clad figure was, and, lowering his eyes, he knew that this, in truth, was the grief upon which no one should intrude.

How long they knelt there, side by side, he wasn't sure. Baldwin's sister, moaning and wailing as if she had just lost the most precious person in her life, and Baldwin's best friend, silent and brave, praying for the repose of his soul. What a contrast!

No one else would ever guess, Geoffrey thought to himself, which was the heart most anguished.

At long last, Her Royal Highness was finished publicizing her mourning and stood abruptly to depart. As she turned away from the coffin, her cloak knocked one of the candlesticks, and it toppled over. The flame instantly went out, but Geoffrey saw a stream of burning wax splatter onto Theo's folded hands. The young Templar, however, didn't move.

One of the sergeants had also seen it and instinctively rose to go forward, but Geoffrey reached out and restrained him.

"Don't," he whispered. "He's all right. Leave him to pray."

The sergeant merely shrugged and knelt back down.

Geoffrey had already started to suspect, of course, way back when he had dug out that arrowhead and Brother Theo had endured the agony with hardly a sound. Yet even then, Geoffrey hadn't been completely sure.

Now he was.

His little brother could no longer feel pain.

∽ Afterword ∾

THE following year, 1186, the child-King Baldwin the Fifth also died, and Guy de Lusignan ascended the Throne.

In July of 1187 Saladin besieged Tiberias. King Guy summoned not only the religious-military Orders, but all the knights in the Kingdom, and, under appalling conditions and against all prudent advice (urged only by Gerard de Ridford), marched his army against the Infidel. The ensuing battle, at a place called the Horns of Hattin, resulted in the most devastating defeat the Christians had ever suffered and was a turning point in the history of the Crusades. Every knight who did not die of thirst in the waterless desert was either slaughtered in battle or sold into slavery. However, Saladin reserved for himself the deadly fate of a select few:

The first was Renaud de Chatillon, the Lord of Kerak. He was captured, taken to the Sultan's tent and personally beheaded by Saladin. No one would ever have dreamed that he was to be the great-great-grandfather of a future saint, Queen Elizabeth of Hungary.

Second, the warrior-monks. So feared were they by the Muslims that they could not be allowed to live, even in slavery. All the surviving Templars, nearly three hundred in number, became the victims of Saladin's calculated cruelty. He assigned to his youngest and most inexperienced swordsmen the task of trying to behead them. Some died quickly; most did not. All died with heroic resignation.

Their Grand Master, Gerard de Ridford, was spared, for, as Saladin put it, his idiotic advice to King Guy had made possible the Muslim victory.

Count Raymond of Tripoli was likewise allowed to live, but he died a few years later. Whether or not he had at one time been a traitor, as history strongly suggests, is known only to God.

Guy de Lusignan was captured, but later released. He obviously posed no threat to Saladin.

The Sultan's army then marched to Jerusalem and, in October of that same year, easily took the city. Victory after victory followed, until most of the Holy Land was eventually back in Infidel hands.

Queen Sibyl died shortly after the fall of Jerusalem, and Guy went on to found the De Lusignan dynasty on the island of Cyprus.

Five more Crusades were launched over the next century in order to reclaim the Holy Land for Christ, including that led by Richard the Lionheart and the noble attempts of the great King Saint Louis of France.

All met with failure.

The Kingdom of Jerusalem has been lost to this day.

⮜ About the Author ⮞

Susan Peck (née Millovitsch) was born in Connecticut, U.S.A. After graduating from St. Mary's Academy, Kansas, in 1985, she tried the religious life in both the Benedictine and Carmelite Orders for several years but, realizing it was not God's will for her, left before taking vows. She is now married and lives in New Zealand, where she and her husband homeschool their nine children.

Mrs. Peek is also the author of several short biographies of saints which have been produced in audio format, as well as a movie screenplay, co-written with her husband Jeff and later adapted into her first novel, *A Soldier Surrenders*.

Susan Peek has a special love for medieval history, in particular the Crusades.